The Diary of Young Arthur Conan Doyle

Sherlock Holmes At
Lincoln's Tomb

Edited by

PROF. RICHARD KREVOLIN

&

DR. JOHN RAFFENSPERGER

Paperback ISBN 978-1-78705-703-6
ePub ISBN 978-1-78705-704-3
PDF ISBN 978-1-78705-705-0

Published in the UK by MX Publishing
335 Princess Park Manor, Royal Drive,
London, N11 3GX
www.mxpublishing.co.uk

Covers painted by Ewa Czarniecka,
graphic design Kyra Dunn, compilation Brian Belanger.

To our esteemed editor, Nancy Cohen; our wonderful agent, Paula Munier; Renee Braeunig; Melanie Jappy; Kathy Copas; Colleen Sell; Dr. Wally Duff; Dr. Glenn Shepard; John Haslett; Penny Macleod; Steve Callender; Katja Bressette; Katia Haddidian; Coach Bob Orgovan, and the Sanibel writing group four.

When an old trunk of Sir Arthur Conan Doyle's personal effects came up for auction at Sotheby's, we eagerly placed a bid and won the lot. The old footlocker contained a most priceless gem. Yes, buried deep inside the rotting wooden chest, under his old medical instruments and clothes, was a series of hand-written journals. And, neatly tucked inside the first journal was this note:

"It is July 7, 1930. I am gravely ill and do not think I will live through the night. And so, it has become incumbent upon me to deal with these four leather-bound journals from my medical school days. I have always treasured them since they reveal the most personal details of the formative moments of my young life.

Due to their private nature, I thought it would be unseemly if they outlived me, so I walked them over to the fireplace in my library. However, as the heat of the flames licked their spines, I was unable to fully carry out my mission.

And so now, I reluctantly place these journals in this old footlocker and hope that these intimate entries are not exploited in a most untasteful way and instead, that one day, they are published in their entirety in order to convey to the world the simple truth about the grand adventures I had with Dr. Bell and Mr. Sherlock Holmes during my medical apprenticeship.

-- Sir Arthur Conan Doyle"

And so, more than one hundred years later, Sir Arthur Conan Doyle's dying wish has finally been fulfilled. You then, dear reader, now hold a "lost diary" of Sir Arthur Conan Doyle, written while he was student at the University of Edinburgh Medical School. Experts have always assumed, as we did, that Dr. Joseph Bell, the Edinburgh surgeon was Conan Doyle's inspiration for Sherlock Holmes. In fact, Conan Doyle was acquainted with a drop-out from a London medical school, named Sherlock Holmes who performed experiments in the laboratory of Dr. Bell as early as 1878. Holmes learned from Dr. Bell how to observe minute details and became a skilled medical diagnostician. He used this Impressive gift to solve crimes and to defend the British Empire. These diaries provide convincing evidence that Arthur Conan Doyle based his fictional detective on a real Sherlock Holmes. This volume details the true story of Doyle's first year of service as the clerk for Dr. Joseph Bell, a gifted diagnostician, as well as detailing the origin of some of Robert Louis Stevenson and J. M. Barrie's most beloved characters.

So now then, we entrust this diary to you, my dear reader. We hope you gain as much pleasure perusing its pages as we did when we first discovered it – there buried deep within the wooden confines of that ancient treasure chest…

-- The Editors: Dr. J. Raffensperger and Prof. Richard Krevolin, 9 October, 2020

25 September, 1878

Students came tumbling in to the surgical amphitheater and elbowed their ways up the tiered seats that overlooked the "cockpit" that had the stench of carbolic and chloroform from the morning's operations. It was Dr. Joseph Bell's Friday afternoon surgical clinic. I was Dr. Bell's clerk, charged with the task of taking a history, performing a cursory examination and making a diagnosis on each patient.

The last man to enter the amphitheater was the new extracurricular student, a tall, very slender fellow who was a few years older than my classmates but had disdained our games and sports. He was quite pale, with thinnish lips and small wrinkles about his dark glittering eyes. He had chemical blotches and burns on his hands. The sleeve of his coat showed permanganate stains and holes that could have been the result of spilled nitric acid. There were rumors that he had been expelled from a hospital in London. He did not mingle with other students but spent many hours in the chemical laboratory, where, it was rumored, he was investigating new surgical antiseptics for Dr. Bell. I had also seen him, late at night, dissecting a fresh cadaver in the anatomy lab. Using a scalpel, he made an incision from the shoulder to the upper arm and immediately laid bare the subclavian artery and the plexus of nerves. The fellow had a strange genius for anatomy as well as chemistry.

I was in the anteroom with the first of the day's patients, a huge brute of a man around forty with a long, red beard that barely hid a hard, pocked face. His shoulders and muscular biceps bulged through a thick woolen shirt, and his black, homespun pants were stuck into mud-stained, cowhide, knee-high boots. He slurred his words and walked with a shuffling gait.

"Your name, please," I asked.

"MacLure."

"What's the matter?"

"It's me fingers," he said.

"Well, what about your fingers?"

"See for yourself."

He held up his right hand. The fourth and fifth fingers turned from a deathly white to blue and then to a dull red color before my eyes.

"Mr. Doyle, my next patient, if you please," Dr. Bell called.

I led Mr. MacLure into the amphitheater and had him sit in a chair directly in front of the students.

Dr. Bell cleared his throat. "Mr. Doyle, you have examined the patient?" he asked.

"Aye."

"We eagerly await your diagnosis."

"From the patient's shuffling gait and slurred speech, he appears to be under the influence of strong drink."

"You observe nothing else?"

"Um, well, well . . . It's his fingers. They change color."

"Is that all?"

"That is not serious, sir?"

"You noted nothing else?"

"Nothing, sir."

"Have you made a diagnosis?"

"No sir."

"What about the tobacco stains on his beard and the ulcer on the top of his right ear?" Bell asked.

I looked at my feet while a classmate chortled. "I don't know, but can't see that they have any connection to his illness."

"Mr. Doyle, for heaven's sake, open your eyes and mind! The tiniest of details might be the key to reaching a proper diagnosis and saving a life. Mr. Holmes, perhaps you can do better than Mr. Doyle."

I stumbled my way into the gallery with my classmates who mumbled sympathy. They could have been in my place. Dammit all! How can I be so dense? Dr. Bell always notices minute details that I miss and draws conclusions that I can never reach.

The new fellow, Holmes, leaped to his feet and in an instant was down in the cockpit, seemingly, quivering with excitement. He took one turn around the patient then stopped and touched MacLure's ear with one long, stained finger. He peered intently at the patient's face and then his hands.

"This is a case of Reynaud's disease and the ulcer is undoubtedly the result of an old case of frostbite. Tobacco aggravates this disease." Holmes said. His gaze fell on a slender leather holster hanging from the patient's belt, flat against his buttock.

Dr. Bell smiled. "You are quite correct," he said.

"Mr. MacLure, are you employed as a gravedigger at Greyfriars?" Holmes asked.

The man's face contorted and his eyes shifted about the room as if seeking an escape. "No, Doctor. Never been near Greyfriars."

Holmes high-pitched voice turned sharp. "The mud on your boots is from the kirkyard. You have lied."

The patient's ruddy face went ghostly pale, and, in a moment, the tips of his fingers turned from blushing red to dead white.

My classmates muttered and twisted in their seats. We were at once astounded and a little jealous of this upstart from London.

Greyfriars? I thought back to last year when several young people had gone missing. They had last been seen walking by Greyfriars Kirkyard. For many months all of Edinburgh was filled with fear of walking at night through that part of town.

"Well, then, Mr. MacLure, if you are not a gravedigger, what is your profession?" Holmes asked.

"I got no job right now."

Holmes thrust a long finger into MacLure's face. "But you once were an iceman on the high lochs?"

"Aye." MacLure's eyebrows went up in surprise. "How did you know?"

"The ice pick in your holster," Holmes said.

Bell rose from his chair and took the patient's right hand. "Thank you Mr. Holmes, excellent deductions. "You noted how his fingers underwent a rapid color change. They turned from red to white and are now changing back to blue. This is, indeed, a sign of Raynaud's disease, named for our French colleague who first observed this phenomenon in 1862. It occurs mainly in women, but also in men who work in the cold or have repetitive injuries to their hands. Damage to the small blood vessels reduces blood flow to the fingers and toes. On warming, an increased flow of blood causes the color changes. Emotional distress, as from telling a lie, also causes the fingers to change color."

Dr. Bell, quick as a cat, reached around the patient and removed a slender steel spike from the holster at his belt. "As Mr. Holmes noted, this is a pick used to divide blocks of ice, aye?"

MacLure did not respond.

Bell held the sharp pointed steel pick in front of MacLure's face. "You were acquainted with Professor Corcoran, were you not?"

"Damn you to hell!" The huge man lunged but Bell neatly stepped away.

Holmes closed both hands into fists, pulled back his right arm and threw a punch that connected with MacLure's nose. There was a spurt of blood, but the huge man merely shook his head. Holmes danced around MacLure, found an opening with a left jab connected with the brute's solar plexus. MacLure made a "woofing" sound but made for the door. He was about to escape when a couple of the other medical students dove onto the brute. MacLure did not budge until two more students plunged down the steps and jumped onto him. The four of them wrestled the giant to the floor of the amphitheatre.

"Call the police!" students cried. MacLure struggled violently until Dr. Bell went behind the brute, grabbed his head, and dramatically held the ice pick at the back on his neck, the point pressing into the flesh. "See here, gentlemen. By inclining the head forward, I can easily press the pick through the foramen magnum at the base of the skull, directly into the medulla oblongata and on into the center of the brain. The victim will die instantly, with no more than a barely detectable pin prick on his neck. An autopsy will demonstrate what appears to be a spontaneous cerebral hemorrhage."

During the tense seconds while Bell held the ice pick tight against MacLure's neck, I remembered the horrible moment in Professor Corcoran's anatomy lab last year when I recognized Allison Davies, a fellow student, on his dissecting table. At first all we saw was her cold, marble-white body, as lovely as the Venus de Milo. Professor Corcoran opened her skull and revealed clots on the surface of her brain. The professor sliced open the brain and found hemorrhaging within the cerebral cortex. In fact, all of Corcoran's cadavers seemed to have brain hemorrhages. Suspicion fell on Corcoran, but, until this moment, there had been no proof of foul play. During Holmes' presentation, I had sunk into a well of despair at my ignorance but the memory of Corcoran's anatomy lab brought up new questions.

I shouted, "Doctor Bell, wait. How is this man related to the cadavers in Professor Corcoran's anatomy laboratory?"

"My dear Doyle. I would wager that our Mr. MacLure was formerly in the employ of Corcoran and is 'The Greyfriars Killer!'"

There was a great hubbub as the students surged down the steps and into the cockpit. MacLure grunted, ducked and made another attempt for the door. Dr. Bell pushed the ice pick deeper into his neck until he drew blood.

Could it be true? If Holmes and Bell were correct, then the bodies in Professor Corcoran's laboratory were the victims of the vicious MacLure. No wonder the professor always had perfect bodies for dissection.

Suddenly, with one final burst of energy, MacLure screamed and threw the boys off and got his hands around Dr. Bell's neck. Holmes cocked his fist and delivered another blow just as a half-dozen police officers burst in and grabbed him. MacLure gave up. The officers dragged the Greyfriars Killer off to prison.

Dr. Bell straightened, cleared his throat, and the smallest hint of a smile etched itself on the side of his mouth. "That is all for today, lads. Thank you very much. Doyle, you and Holmes stay for a minute or two."

My classmates filed out of the room, leaving me, the new man and Dr. Bell.

"Mr. Doyle, don't feel bad. This was a difficult case and you are still young. Meet Mr. Sherlock Holmes who is searching out new chemicals with antiseptic properties." I shook hands with Holmes. His slender hand had a steel grip. "You throw a hard punch. Do you box?" I asked.

Holmes inclined his head with a slight smile. "A bit in school," he said.

"I watched you dissect the brachial plexus. It was extraordinary work. Are you also a surgeon?"

"No, it would be more accurate to say that I am a student of surgery and many other things as well," Holmes replied.

Just then, a messenger arrived with a letter for the Dr. Bell. The stained envelope was marked 'URGENT'.

"This is most unsettling. The envelope was postmarked in Chicago on July 11, yet it only just arrived today," Dr. Bell said.

He slit open the envelope and scanned the letter.

"You two, read this," said he.

Dear Dr. Joseph Bell,

As the President of the Board of Trustees of Rush Medical College, I wish to cordially invite you to perform a series of lectures and demonstrations on the antiseptic surgical techniques practised in Edinburgh. These lectures will inaugurate the mid-term which begins on October 12. An honorarium of one thousand pounds sterling will be paid to you upon completion of these lectures and we shall also cover food, travel, and lodging for you and an assistant. I am enclosing steamship and rail tickets for your journey from Glasgow to Chicago. You may bring an assistant.

I also wish to retain your professional services on a personal matter. As you know, I own one of the largest railroad companies in America. My entrprise is under attack by a unknown person or persons. I pray that you can be of some assistance to me in solving this perplexing mystery.

Yours, very sincerely,

Angus Duncan, Chairman of the Board of Trustees

"Mr. Doyle, what is strange about this letter, aside from the rather lengthy delay in its delivery?"

I re-read the letter. "Um ... Eh ... Nothing I can see, sir. It appears to be an ordinary invitation."

"Mr. Holmes, what do you make of this? Anything unusual?" Bell asked.

"The upstroke on the letters 'L' and 'H' in the second paragraph are thicker, indicating the author applied firmer pressure to the pen. Also in the second paragraph, the word 'enterprise' is misspelt. The author's hand trembled when he signed his name. And why did he use the word 'solving' rather than diagnosing? I deduce that he suspects foul play and fears for his life." Holmes said.

"Exactly," Bell cried.

I examined the letter again. Holmes' keen ability to analyze handwriting had enabled him to detect slight elements which I had missed.

"Angus Duncan was my classmate at the Academy. He was a bit of a scoundrel and the black sheep of his family, but, upon emigrating to America, he made a fortune during the Civil War and is now a respectable railroad baron. I can set aside a month for a trip to America, but no more. It may take more time to solve his mystery." His face creased into a huge smile. "I have a perfect solution. The two of you must accompany me. Doyle, you know my methods and you, Holmes, have a knack for detective work. If I must leave before we solve Duncan's mystery, the two of you can stay on and incidentally share the thousand pounds." Dr. Bell said.

He then studied the steamship tickets. "These tickets are for the *Devonia* that sails from Glasgow on the morning tide to-morrow," Dr. Bell said.

He consulted his gold pocket watch. "And we have missed the last train to Glasgow. Doyle, Holmes, be quick — there is not a moment to lose. Harry will drive us."

"But, sir. It is more than sixty miles, and I have my studies," I said.

"You will learn more in America and, Mr. Doyle, you are my clerk. If we act post-haste, we can make it in time."

He swept up his leather instrument case and was out of the door onto Lauriston Street. In an instant he spotted Harry, his footman, waiting in a barouche carriage. "Home, Harry, with great alacrity . . . Mr. Doyle, Mr. Holmes, get in. Quick, quick."

"I am happy to accompany you, but I must go to my lodgings first," Holmes said.

"But, Dr. Bell, I can't afford to leave my mother," I said.

"Aye, ye can. I'll pay you a stipend for your time. I shall give your mother your entire year's clerkship salary in advance. You will finally be free from worry about money. Where is your sense of adventure, laddie? At your age you should be ripe for a journey," Dr. Bell said.

He had me there. I had always yearned to go on a grand adventure and to try my hand at being like my heroes in the adventure books. How could I refuse such an opportunity?

Our carriage dashed past the castle in a drizzling rain, then on to Princes Street where old ladies were still selling pies to students under the gas lights. Harry whipped up the matched bays and we were off to Dr. Bell's grand residence at 20 Melville Place. Holmes leaned forward with an air of eagerness that I lacked. Within minutes, we reached his home. Dr. Bell lurched to the door with his unsteady gait, the result of nerve damage from diphtheria that he had contracted from a young patient.

He was no sooner through his front door when he shouted for his valet. "Willum, pack the Gladstone bag and my steamer trunk. We shall be gone for a month." He thrust a handful of bills into Harry's hand. "Take young Mr. Doyle and Mr. Holmes to their lodgings. Be quick!"

I felt like the Prince of Wales as I sat with Dr. Bell's footman in the open carriage while it raced through the yellowish fog of *Auld Reekie*. Holmes lit up a curved Meerschaum pipe and puffed away with great nonchalance. "Whoa! Whoa!" Harry yelled ten minutes later, as he stopped the horses in front our squalid rented rooms on Heriot Row. I was barely out of the carriage, when Harry whipped up the horses and rolled away to Holmes' lodgings.

I flung open the front door. Maw was home, but my Da was probably at the pub getting stinking drunk. "Maw, I am going to America with Dr. Bell," I said. "Arthur, but what about your studies? "Dr. Bell said that I'll learn more in one month in America than I would in two at years in school."

"But, how will you pay—"

"Dr. Bell promised me a stipend. I must hurry and pack."

I had only the clothes on my back, but Maw found an extra undershirt and her home-knitted heavy wool stockings, and gave me her bright red wool scarf. I put my meager belongings into a cloth bag along with Macaulay's *History of England*, Cooper's *The Last of The Mohicans*, and a collection of short stories by Edgar Allan Poe. I also packed a blank notebook so I could record my experiences with Dr. Bell. Perhaps, one day, I will have material for stories. Maw also scrounged up my favorite things to eat—a few apples, a pear, a box of sardines, and a packet of butterscotch candies.

I left, but ran back in to give my Maw a big hug. She cried, but I pecked her cheek with a kiss. "I love you, Maw. Thanks," I said.

The carriage was already at the curb, beneath the gaslight. I climbed in, but at least half of the seat was occupied with Holmes' portmanteau, a large canvas bag and an instrument case. I squeezed into the front seat. Harry whipped up the matched bay horses and we were back at Dr. Bell's home in minutes.

The doctor was in the library, before an open gun cabinet, loading a stubby British Bull Dog revolver and a handful of .442 caliber cartridges. It was a deadly weapon at short range. "Is that really necessary?" I asked.

"I daresay we may encounter ruffians in Chicago," he said, while carefully hiding the gun in a compartment of his instrument case.

We lay our bags and a wicker basket on the floor of the carriage. Dr. Bell and I squeezed into the front seat and covered ourselves with a rug. Harry gave a command and we went at a trot through the streets of Edinburgh. When we reached the macadam roadway, Harry urged the horses to a gallop.

Dr. Bell wore his customary top hat and a heavy black overcoat that was useful for his cold trips to the country to care for his patients. Holmes was snuggly clad in a heavy Inverness cape coat and a deerstalker wool cap with earflaps, unusual raiment for a student. I was more and more curious about this strange man. We were beyond the city, and galloping furiously through open country, when he extinguished his beautifully carved Meerschaum pipe, slouched down, and went fast to sleep.

My thick tweed coat repelled the drizzling rain like a duck's downy feathers, but cold water seeped in around my collar and, soon, I shivered from the wet and cold. I pulled Maw's old scarf tighter, and, after a while, drowsed off.

I was awakened by Dr. Bell's voice. "An extra guinea if you change the horses within five minutes." We had stopped at a livery stable to exchange our exhausted horses for a new team. With straw sticking out of his hair, and rubbing sleep from his eyes, the stable boy brought out new horses. Within five minutes, we were on our way. Holmes had awakened. His dark eyes, lit by a flash of the carriage light were alive with a strange eager enthusiasm that I could not share.

Dr. Bell opened the wicker basket and removed a silver flask and a quantity of foodstuffs wrapped in a napkin.

"My dear companions, a sip of this may warm your weary bones."

I waved it off. After seeing what liquor had done to my father over the years I had made a vow never to take a drop of spirits.

"Ah, laddie, a wee dram is good for the body and soul," said he.

He was right. A sip of the malt whisky warmed my stomach. Suddenly, I was ravenous. My last meal had been oatmeal and milk at breakfast, almost a day ago.

"My maw packed a snack," said I.

"Save it for later. My cook packed these viands for our journey."

I started on a chicken leg and then devoured a sandwich. By the time I had finished smoked salmon and rum cake, we were nearing the outskirts of Glasgow. It was still many a mile to the steamship docks on the Clyde. Holmes accepted a dram of the whiskey, but only nibbled at a bit of chicken.

The Tollbooth tower clock struck five as we trotted through Glasgow Cross. Dr. Bell shouted, "Harry, faster! The ship leaves on the tide."

We were not going to make it. Harry bellowed and cursed at the horses. I prayed that the ship might leave a few minutes late.

At last, we reached the docks as the eastern sky grew lighter. I was barely able to make out the black funnel of our ship amongst the masts and derricks.

"*Devonia*, hold for special passengers. HOLD GODDAMNIT!!!" Harry commanded, with a thunderous shout.

He whipped up the tired horses for the final dash, and we arrived just as the dockhands were releasing the hawsers that held the gangplank.

Dr. Bell gave five guineas to Harry. "You've done wonders tonight. I am deeply grateful. Get yourself a pint, some food and rest," said he.

He would not trust the instrument case to the ship's men. "Doyle take charge of the instrument case. Don't let it out of your sight, Dr. Bell said. I toiled up the gangplank and at the top was stopped dead by the sight of a pale and lovely face looking out at the dock.

Sad, tearful green eyes. Flaming red hair hanging in ringlets about her pale, delicate features. A lovely, ethereal angel.

The most beautiful creature I had ever seen was standing before me.

And then, she waved.

My heart raced.

Of all the men on the ship, she chose to wave at me!

I smiled, and, as I was about to wave back, I sadly realized that she was waving at a lad of no more than twelve years who happened to be standing on the dock right behind me.

"Miss Yates, stop that mewling. Jimmy needs you this instant," a sharp, gruff voice suddenly intoned.

She turned and disappeared. What was I thinking? My medical studies came first. I had no time for women. In the meantime, Holmes generously tipped a stevedore, who hauled his gear aboard ship.

The second officer at the head of the gangplank was respectful but spoke to Dr. Bell quite forcefully. "Sir, this ticket is for one first class stateroom, but there are three in your party," he said.

"A mere last minute change of plans. I am sure you can accommodate us," Bell said, with an equally firm tone. He was not one to have his wishes disobeyed.

"Well, it is fortunate that we have a single, first class cabin. It is small, but quite comfortable one person," said the purser.

"Capital, I would prefer a single room. My few small experiments might offend another person," said Holmes.

"Then it is settled, Doyle, there is no time to dawdle. Hurry along and take my instrument case to our cabin."

26 September, 1878

By the time Dr. Bell and I settled in our cramped quarters my wet clothing left puddles of water on our stateroom floor. I sneezed and had a fit of shivering as I carefully stowed the instrument case beneath Dr. Bell's bunk and then collapsed onto my own.

I was cold, wet, and tired, yet, for the first time in a year, I was free from the Edinburgh Infirmary and the pressures of university. I was grateful for the change. For a few days, I would be a man of leisure.

The purser, a muscular black man, brought Dr. Bell's Gladstone bag, trunk, and my cloth bag.

With a flourish, he unpacked the trunk and arranged Dr. Bell's clothing in our closet. He then removed my shirt and the extra stockings from my bag and stacked my books on a small shelf. He did all of this with a genuine smile on his face. When he was finished, he turned to me with a quizzical look. "Is this all, sir?" he asked.

"Aye, that's it. What is your name?" I inquired.

"My name is Bub, once a slave, but a freeman now. Sirs, the first gong will announce breakfast after the ship is underway." Dr. Bell gave him a shilling while I struggled out of my wet coat.

"Good heavens, Mr. Doyle, have you no dry clothing?"

"Only a shirt and a pair of stockings, sir."

"We are first-class passengers. You can't go about looking like a pauper, laddie."

But, I am a pauper, and a dirt poor one at that, but no laddie. I am a man of almost twenty-years! Why did Bell always ride me so hard? "Try these," he said, just as I was about to make a tart response. He took a dark green wool jacket and grey trousers from the closet.

We were of about the same height, both over six feet tall, but, from playing rugger and boxing, I had more muscle. The coat was tight across the shoulders, but, left unbuttoned, the fit was not too bad and the trousers were perfect.

I felt like a true gentleman, rather than a poor student, and was instantly ashamed of myself. The professor had a streak of humanity after all. Warmth returned. "Thank you, sir," I managed to say, after a fit of sneezing.

The ship's engine rumbled, and a great blast from its horn announced the *Devonia*'s progress down the Clyde. A gong sounded with a sharp *clang*. "That is for breakfast," I said.

"I am not the least hungry." Dr. Bell laid out writing material, his books and papers on the small desk under our porthole and set to work on revising his manual of surgery.

The first-class saloon in the middle section of the ship was as fine as any gentleman's club. There were tables for six. Wood paneling and portraits of great ships lined the walls. Off-duty ship's officers were at one table, but it was early and there were only a few other diners. Holmes was nowhere to be seen.

I had no sooner selected a table where I could be alone with my whirling thoughts about Dr. Bell and that red-haired girl when a white-coated waiter poured a cup of strong tea from a silver pot and left a tray of toast and marmalade.

This was followed by rashers of bacon, fried and boiled eggs, potatoes, a mutton chop, and kippered herrings. I felt obliged to eat everything, and, out of a sense of duty and moral obligation, I also forced down an apple tart, a pear tart, and another cup of tea.

The ship was vibrating as we steamed with the tide down the River Clyde. The wind that blew across the deck was invigorating, but, after the long night and hearty meal, I could not fight off drooping eyelids and a feeling of lassitude.

I journeyed back to our cabin. Dr. Bell was inside, reading and chewing on a gangly ginger root. I climbed into the upper bunk.

27 September, 1878

I slept until well past noon yesterday, and awoke to a peculiarly unpleasant sensation in the pit of my stomach. Dr. Bell was still at the small desk, his legs stretched out, while he read from a textbook of surgery and wrote a few lines on a sheet of foolscap. The entire room was rolling, and even the papers and ink pot on the desk slid from one side to the other with the ship's motion.

"Tsk, tsk, young Doyle. You slept away the best part of the day. We are well out in the Firth of Clyde and shall soon round the Mull of Kintyre to the North Channel."

I hardly heard his words when I was overcome with the two terrible sensations of whirling about and nausea. I tried swallowing back the copious amounts of spit and acid, but they kept coming back up. I made it to the side of the ship just in time.

My prodigious breakfast splashed into the sea. For the rest of the day and night I gagged and heaved into a bucket provided by the gentle purser, Bub.

"Ah, my boy, you should know ginger root is a capital remedy for *mal de mer*, but it is only effective as a preventative, not as a cure," said Dr. Bell.

By this afternoon, we were well out in the Atlantic Ocean and the ship was steadier. I held down a spot of tea and set out on unsteady feet for a walk. Passengers were lounging on deck chairs covered by heavy blankets, but there was no sign of the red-haired girl.

I then ventured onto the more crowded second-class deck and down a series of ladders to steerage, where hundreds of poor emigrants slept in their clothing on hard tiers of shelves. The noise and stink of vomit and unwashed bodies was unbearable. *This is where I really belong*, I thought, and, for a moment, I was ready to abandon my first-class cabin.

There was no sign of that wonderful and mysterious red-haired girl.

Back on the open deck, I filled my lungs with a bit of fresh air and felt better. I even thought about food once again. Halfway down the port side, just aft of the funnel, I came across a lanky, pale fellow with long brown hair and a wispy mustache wearing a stained velvet coat. He was resting on a nest of coiled rope and canvas, scribbling in a notebook, with his face to the warm sun. It took me a moment to recognize him — he was an old mate who had been several years ahead of me at Edinburgh University.

"Stevenson, old fellow, what are you doing here?"

"Arthur, I could say the same to you, old sod." Robert Louis Stevenson swept away a lock of dark hair that hung over his eyes.

"You first, and then I'll tell my tale."

"I'm off to California to meet the woman I love. What about you?"

"I'm with Dr. Joseph Bell, a faculty member at Edinburgh. I am his outpatient clerk, although, sometimes, I feel more like his valet than a medical assistant. The doctor is to give lectures in America.

"A fellow named Holmes, Sherlock Holmes, a chemist, is with us as well. Ever heard of him?"

Stevenson rubbed his chin and his faced screwed up into a frown. "Ah, yes, I have heard of a man named Holmes. He was at school with a friend of mine. By all accounts he was hardly a pleasant sort, kept to himself, but was a brilliant student — studied a bit of everything, but never finished his classes. Dr. Bell, well, he is a great surgeon, second only to Lister himself. And Lister, you know, helped my dear friend, William Ernest Henley, the poet. London doctors had amputated one of his legs for tuberculosis of the bone and wanted to take his other leg as well. Lister kept poor Henley in bed and saved his one leg with surgery and carbolic dressings. Your field is dreadfully gory, Arthur."

Stevenson's face turned unusually pale, and he was wracked with a deep cough. He got up from his nest and barely made it to the railing to spit out a gob of yellow mucous. The poor man was little more than skin and bone and appeared to be deathly ill. "I prefer the gilded fantasy of fiction," said he.

"I remember seeing you with Henley on the surgical wards. Weren't you studying law then?" I asked.

"Engineering first, and then the law, aye. All the while, though, I felt as if I were lost upon the seven seas. A man without a calling . . . But, you, my dear friend, don't seem to have that problem. Your true love is the medical arts, aye?"

"Well, medical school has been a long, weary grind of botany, chemistry, anatomy, physiology, and subjects that seem to have little bearing upon the art of curing."

"Ah yes, the dull, mind-numbing grind of studies . . . Why do you think I am here and not back there?"

"In all honesty, I yearn for adventure and dream of sitting at my desk and penning famous tales like Poe, but that will never happen. I come from a humble background and shall practise medicine so that I will always have two pence to pay the taxman."

"Quite the pragmatic choice, but . . . I prefer your dream life . . . To be able to support oneself only through the might of the pen. That would be a dream come true."

I gestured to the men swarming up the mast, setting the sails to catch the following breeze. "Well then, mate, why don't you write of this adventure? Spice it up a bit with some buried treasure and pirates, and I'll wager you might garner the interest of a London publishing house," said I.

"I could not. I haven't the skills nor imagination."

"Then, like Shakespeare himself, base your characters on real figures, such as Henley."

He coughed. "What do you mean?"

"Henley, with his wooden leg, could serve as the model for a murderous pirate. Can't you just hear the thump of his stump on a tavern floor or the deck of a sailing ship?"

"I would not want to offend poor Henley, especially after he's been through so much."

"You need not worry if you alter his character a bit. Make up a fitting moniker. Let us see . . . With only one leg, you might call him something like 'Short John' and give him a murderous craving for silver coin."

"Hmmm . . . That is a thought worth considering. I often carry pencil and paper with the hope of someday capturing a good yarn." Poor Stevenson had another fit of coughing.

"And you might also consider consulting with Dr. Bell about your lungs."

"You sawbones are all alike. The doctors in France recommended a year at bed rest and the Germans prescribed hot baths. It is all tomfoolery. For me, the prescription's simple — travel, a warm woman, and a hot climate. I do not intend to waste away in bed, but will live as I like and shall die with my boots on."

"I see. And speaking of women, Robert, have you spied a lovely lass with wild red hair on the ship?"

"Ah yes, Arthur. I see that working with Dr. Bell has also helped your powers of observation."

"Do you know her, by chance?"

"I do."

"So tell, my friend . . . Tell all."

"I would, but I do apologize. I have a pressing engagement." He started to get up. I grabbed him by the forearm and implored him with a stare and my firm grip. "I give in . . . Her name is Rebecca.

Rebecca Yates. She is a nurse to the spoiled brat son of a Presbyterian minister."

"By the name of?"

"James Balfour. The insufferable man is a distant cousin of my mother and recently dismissed from a church in Aberdeen. "

"I see . . . Hmmm . . ."

"Oh, Arthur, do join me tomorrow night for the evening's entertainment in the companionway between steerage three and four."

"I can't make it. I must be sure to study my medical texts and keep my diary up to date."

"Dear, misguided Arthur, put your beloved books aside and live. It should be quite a frolic. I promise such a bevy of busty lassies. You'll soon forget red-haired Rebecca."

"We shall see." I smiled and bid Robert farewell.

I took another turn around the deck, breathing fresh air and observing the ocean's waves. I had not seen Holmes since coming aboard, so I knocked at the door to his stateroom. "The door is open, do come in," he called. Great clouds of blue tobacco smoke filled the small room. Holmes was at a small desk, dressed in an ornate dressing gown, puffing his curved Meerschaum pipe and tinkering with test tubes. He said not a word of greeting, but exclaimed, "Doyle, do look at this tube — dissolved crystals of iodine in alcohol — this could be a better antiseptic in surgical wounds than phenol." There was a stack of books by the desk and bottles of chemicals. This explained the great amount of luggage he carried. "Yes, interesting," I said. He made no further comment, but went to mixing various chemicals in tubes. "I shall be getting along," I said.

28 September, 1878

After the evening meal I scribbled down the day's events, read for a few hours, but needed a break, so I met Stevenson in his second-class cabin just forward of the companionway. His room was little more than an open space in the deckhouse, lit by a wildly swinging lantern. Through a side door there were glimpses of the night sea. Couples were already whirling about, dancing to the music of a fiddle.

Down below on the first landing, near coils of rope and a huge capstan, a half-dozen Irish girls danced a lively jig. Stevenson was right. Several of them caught my attention, but their green eyes never rested on me. They were more interested in the sailors. After a few pints of beer, I was eager for a dance or a kiss, but those thoughts were unworthy of Rebecca. And, besides, the lassies had picked out their sailors.

The evening wore on, and the company grew to at least thirty or forty people, including a few from the first-class cabins. The fiddler played a bastard doggerel from the music halls accompanied by onlookers keeping time by beating tin pans with spoons.

As the evening came to a close, a particularly comely Irish girl, with painted lips and a saucy smile, climbed on the capstan and danced to a rousing jig. She kicked up her legs and, at the end, turned her back on the audience, flung up her skirt, and aimed her backside at the audience. There was wild applause and shouts of "More! More!" but, at that very moment, the bosun arrived. "All turn in!" he bellowed.

I bid Stevenson a bleary "Good night," and staggered back to my cabin.

29 September, 1878

After only a few hours of sleep, during the deep dark of night, I was awakened by beating on our door. Dr. Bell, in his nightclothes, opened the door to reveal the ship's Captain and two armed sailors.

"Dr. Bell, sir, sorry to trouble you at this ungodly hour. Would you be so kinds as to see a gravely ill passenger?" the Captain asked.

Dr. Bell threw his heavy overcoat over his night clothing, while I quickly donned my tweed jacket. The wind had come up again, and as we made our way to the passenger's cabin, we were assaulted by sea spray. Clouds closed in on the ship's masts making the night even gloomier.

The victim was the same Irish girl who had danced so madly on the capstan only a few hours ago. The swinging lanterns provided only a fitful light, but one of the sailors produced a bullseye lamp to illuminate her body. The poor girl's swollen, black tongue protruded between her lips, and her eyes bulged as if in mortal fear. There was no pulse or heartbeat, but the body was still warm.

"She is well beyond my care," Dr. Bell said.

"I thought as much. Can you determine the cause of death?" asked the Captain.

The skin on her neck was red, badly abraded, and her throat was almost cut through just beneath her jaw.

"Death was certainly due to strangulation. Note the twist marks. I should think she was attacked from behind. The murderer used a twisted chain or heavy cord about an eighth of an inch in diameter," Dr. Bell said.

There was another strange finding. Her bodice was open, and written with the girl's own lip paint across her breasts was the word "Tzabel." Neither of us, for all our study of Latin, Greek, and French, knew the word. It was a mystery.

"Captain, I suggest that you maintain absolute secrecy about the mode of death and this word," Dr. Bell said.

His head was sunk in thought while I made ready for bed. "It is unlikely that an ignorant sailor committed this crime. I believe the murder was the work of an educated man. We must bring Holmes into this," said he.

4 October, 1878

Nothing eventful has occurred over the past few days, thus, I have not written any new entries here. Today, fresh rumors are flying about the ship. Many passengers are certain that a crewman committed the fiendish murder. Women will not walk about the decks alone, and even the men have taken to carrying personal weapons.

This morning, I paid a courtesy visit to the sick bay in the hope of furthering my education in regards to the practice of medicine at sea. The ship's doctor was a trembling American with a purple nose and broken veins in his cheeks. One glance at his untidy desk and nearly empty medicine cabinet told the story of a man long gone to drink. As I looked at him and his quarters, I tried not to think of my own Da.

The ship's doctor gave heroic doses of mercury to the crew for their chronic venereal disease and prescribed opium in alcohol for the passengers so that they might sleep through the voyage.

Desperate for better care, several passengers requested a consultation with Dr. Bell. These culminated in Bub bringing a request for Dr. Bell to see a sick child. My heart quickened when I saw that the note was signed by none other than a Mrs. James Balfour.

I followed the good doctor, carrying his black medicine bag, hoping to meet or at least see Miss Rebecca Yates. When Miss Yates, herself, opened the door, I was overcome, turned red in the face, and lost the power of speech.

Dr. Bell bowed and introduced himself to the Reverend Balfour and to his wife. I stood, blushing, holding the black bag. "My capable assistant, Mr. Arthur Conan Doyle," said he.

The minister was a mild-mannered, meek man of about forty who stood aside while his wife wiped tears from her eyes and showed us to the bedside of their five-year-old son. Her deeply lined face was creased with worry and she wrung her hands. "Oh Doctor, thank you for coming. Poor Jimmy hasn't had a moment's rest. I fear it is typhoid."

I would never have noticed, but Dr. Bell's eyes were immediately drawn to the heavy twisted gold watch chain that crossed the minister's chest from one vest pocket to another.

"Has anyone in the family been ill? Reverend Balfour, do you feel well?" Dr. Bell asked.

"I was a trifle indisposed last night, but am quite well this morning."

"Just to be sure, I should check your pulse. May I use your watch?"

"Certainly."

The Reverend Balfour snapped open his heavy gold watch and passed the instrument with its peculiar chain to Dr. Bell, who ostentatiously held the man's wrist while counting his pulse. I was puzzled when Dr. Bell ran a fingernail over the length of the gold chain. Had he, with his famous powers of observation, noted a detail that I had missed?

"Your pulse is quite normal. May I ask a question?"

"Of course," the minister said.

"Are you acquainted with the word Tzabel? T-z-a-b-e-l?"

"That is old Hebrew for Jezebel, an evil woman, the wife of Ahab, in First and Second Kings." There was no trace of nervousness or anxiety in his voice. Reverend Balfour could have been preaching a sermon.

Suddenly, a look of comprehension passed over Dr. Bell's face. Had he deduced who the killer was?

Jimmy made a most piteous cry, demanding attention. Dr. Bell did not speak, but sat by the boy, chin on his hand, and turned his penetrating gaze to the lad. Without a word, he placed his hand on the boy's abdomen. Jimmy clenched his eyes and writhed in pain.

I was certain the poor child was suffering from the last stages of peritonitis when Jimmy half opened one eye to peer about the room. Then, when he thought no one was looking, a brief smile came over his face as if he were having a grand old time being the center of attention.

Dr. Bell probed his abdomen for an enlarged liver or spleen, then counted the pulse. "Young man, please open your mouth and stick out your tongue."

"What did he eat last evening?"

"He cleaned his plate of beef, potatoes, gravy, bread, milk, and a bit of pie. We all had the same meal, but it couldn't have been the food," his mother said.

"When did he have the raspberry jam and chocolate?" Bell asked.

"We never allow him to have sweets."

Dr. Bell wiped his finger across the edge of the lad's mouth and displayed a sticky red smear with tell-tale raspberry seeds. Next, he held up the lad's right hand. "If you will, Mrs. Balfour, please sample this brown substance on his right index finger. It is chocolate, a Dutch chocolate if I am not mistaken."

I had peered over his shoulder and had seen none of these clues. Again, I felt like an oaf, unfit to practice medicine.

"Your son's greedy, that's all. He's a glutton. Give him a dose of castor oil and no food for the rest of the day," said Dr. Bell, with an uncharacteristically harsh tone. He was usually so gentle with children.

The mild-mannered Reverend Balfour was suddenly transformed. His once-placid face became contorted into a dark rictus of hatred. His lips pulled back, exposing yellowing teeth, and his eyes sunk into slits buried within horrid wrinkles. In an instant he had become a beast — an aged, horrid beast with outstretched, claw-like fingers.

Balfour took up a sewing case and swung it with all his might at Dr. Bell's head. "Damned bloody bastard! No one calls my son a glutton."

Dr. Bell ducked, and the sewing case smashed against the wall of the cabin, where it splintered—sending needles and thread flying about the room. The Reverend Balfour swayed as if he would fall, but, then, lurched across the small room towards Rebecca. "It was you, witch! You gave him the chocolate!" His scream ended with a hideous choking and gurgling in his throat.

I blocked him before he reached the poor girl, who had collapsed into a heap against the wall. Then, we watched in horror as the minister's right arm jerked with uncontrollable spasms and his right leg collapsed.

He fell to the floor with his legs jerking convulsively. Powerful neck muscles, contracting like iron bars, pulled his head backwards until I thought his neck would dislocate. He lapsed into unconsciousness.

As his mouth clenched tightly and his breathing became labored, Dr. Bell urged, "Doyle, open his mouth. Don't let his tongue fall back."

What was I supposed to do? I hesitated and trembled when Rebecca handed me a spoon. I stood there, doing nothing, until she grabbed the spoon, jammed it through the clenched teeth, and pried open the man's mouth. I pulled myself together and grasped his slobbery tongue. His breathing became less labored.

"A light. I need a light, please." Dr. Bell said.

Rebecca lit a candle, which the doctor held before the sick man's eyes. The pupil of his right eye contracted normally in response to the light, but there was no reaction in the left eye. "The fact that his left pupil doesn't contract in the light doesn't bode well. Has he had these spells in the past or complained of headaches?"

Mrs. Balfour sobbed uncontrollably and could not answer. "He has suffered unbearable headaches for the past year and has had similar, though milder, spells," said Rebecca. "Dr. Balfour was dismissed from his church when he had an attack during a service and smashed the altar," she barely whispered.

The epileptic fit had passed, but the Reverend Balfour was in a deep coma. His tongue no longer fell back in his throat, but he struggled to breathe, with harsh, labored gasps. Dr. Bell again knelt by the man and carefully probed the left side of his head. "Mr. Doyle, feel this."

There was the slightest elevation and irregularity of the scalp above and behind his left eye forward of the ear. "What is it, sir?" I asked.

"Elementary," said Dr. Bell. "This is a case of Jacksonian epilepsy, caused by a tumor pressing on his brain. I fear he is hemorrhaging from the tumor. We must elevate the bone to relieve the pressure on the brain and, if possible, remove the tumor."

Dr. Bell rose to his height. "We must operate immediately. Have the sick bay scrubbed with carbolic until it is sparkling clean. We will need freshly laundered, boiled linen." Under the circumstances, I could not understand how he was so calm and determined.

"But, sir, trephining the skull is dangerous, even in a hospital."

"Believe, me this is for the best. Please ask Mr. Holmes to attend," said he.

Rebecca commandeered two housekeepers to scrub the sick bay walls and floor with strong soap. I washed the operating table and a desk for the instruments with dilute carbolic acid.

Dr. Bell ordered the Captain to slow the ship and put her on a stable course.

"Damn, we will be late to New York!" the angry red-faced Captain spluttered.

"It is the law of the sea. You must obey a doctor when there is a medical emergency," Dr. Bell said.

Bub and another purser carried the unconscious man to the newly scrubbed sick bay and, as gently as any nurse, placed him on the table with the left side of his head uppermost. A moment later, Dr. Bell walked in and his face fell. The small room was only illuminated by a tiny porthole. "This'll never do. There's too little light for a delicate operation."

Stevenson, sensing a possible story, had slipped into the sick bay. "Dr. Bell, if you will, I have an idea."

"And who, exactly, are you, lad?"

"Robert Louis Stevenson, at your service. I have a bit of experience with lighting and would like to try something if you'll allow me . . . Doyle, hand me those oil lanterns and that looking glass."

Dr. Bell grew interested. "Hmm . . . Aye, but Stevenson, can you create a bright light?"

"We shall see," Stevenson said as he placed four lanterns on a shelf above the operating table. With a calculating eye, he placed the mirror in front of the lanterns, which he angled down to concentrate light at the patient's head.

"Stevenson, where did you learn that ingenious trick?" I asked.

"I'm from a family of lighthouse engineers and I even gave a paper on mirrors and light to the Royal Society." He turned up the flames, bathing the patient's head in light as if he was outdoors on a sunny day. Amazing!

Bell ran his hands through the bright light. "Quite ingenious."

I set out the scalpels, chisels, trephine, forceps, needles, and stitches, all freshly soaked in carbolic, on a clean white sheet. We then rolled up our sleeves and scrubbed our hands with a mild carbolic solution. Balfour roused out of his deep coma, mumbled incoherently and tried to rise up from the table. Mr. Sherlock Holmes arrived, as if on cue. "Mr. Holmes have you administered anesthetics?" Bell asked.

"Yes, on many occasions," Holmes replied.

Was this more braggadocio? Was the man really so talented? I wondered. Without a word, Holmes folded a small towel into a cone and with great dexterity poured a few drops of chloroform and held the towel beneath Balfour's nose. Our patient took a few shallow breaths and coughed. Holmes poured a few more drops. Balfour inhaled deeply and relaxed. It was an admirable display of the anesthetic art.

"You many commence the operation at any time," Holmes said.

"Lassie, can you thread needles?" Dr. Bell asked.

"I have threaded needles since I was five years old," Miss Rebecca Yates replied.

"Good. Thread the needles with silk and keep the instruments in good order," he replied.

Bub, clearly a man of many talents shaved and washed the minister's head. It shone in the bright light.

"Holmes, if you please, hold his head, like so, with the left side uppermost. It must remain steady. Mr. Doyle see to the bleeding," Bell said.

I could not for the life of me remember the location of the temporal lobe. But, fortunately, Dr. Bell knew exactly what he was doing.

He studied the head as if it were a laboratory specimen. After a moment, he took up a scalpel, and, gently, with its tip, marked the line of incision on the scalp. It was curved above and just forward of an imaginary line drawn between the eye and the ear. "Doyle, press with all your might down on either side of the incision, please."

This was a job usually reserved for senior surgical house officers. I had never assisted at an operation and felt bile rising in my throat. My right hand trembled when blood trickled from the scratch.

"Doyle, there is no time to dilly dally. Buck up, lad. Press on the scalp."

Well, I thought, I will use my muscle. After years of playing rugby I was strong. I pressed as hard as possible. There was hardly any bleeding. From the semi-circular scalp incision, he stitched an artery and laid back the scalp to expose an irregular area of bone.

The trephine was little more than a carpenter's brace connected to a round bit designed to bore through bone. When he had made three openings down to the membranes surrounding the brain, he connected the holes with a hammer and chisel.

His only words were, "Bub, if you please, hold the head as still as possible."

Though just a beginning student, I could identify the hard grey tumor that bulged up from the membranes covering the brain. Bell cut around the tumor until the gyri and sulci of the temporal lobe of the brain came into view.

I was completely carried away by seeing a functioning human brain inside a living man's skull. Dr. Bell jolted me out of my reverie. "Please Doyle, help. I can't see to do my work unless you mop away the blood."

With fifteen minutes of concentrated work using forceps and knife, he removed the plum-sized tumor and dropped it into a metal tray.

Dr. Bell used firm pressure and a few stitches to stop blood that trickled from open veins on the surface of the brain. Every time he held out his hand for more stitches, Miss Yates had the needle threaded and ready.

He replaced the bone, sutured the scalp, and applied the carbolic dressings. It was over. I had concentrated so hard on the operation, I forgot my distress, and although my legs trembled, I had passed a milestone in my medical career. Holmes had stopped giving chloroform, but the patient remained asleep.

Miss Yates took her leave to care for Mrs. Balfour and Jimmy. Dr. Bell sent word to the Captain that all was well. Soon, we were steaming at top speed on our original course. Holmes with scarcely a word took his leave. It appeared that he cared little about the patient. A strange, cold hearted man, I thought.

Dr. Bell insisted that our patient remain on the sick bay table until he awoke from his coma. He watched over the unconscious man with brooding eyes. It was near midnight when Stevenson strolled in with a flask of French brandy. He listened to my worried query.

"Dr. Bell, will you notify the Captain about your suspicions of Reverend Balfour? He is surely the murderer."

He gave me a queer look. "The murderer is gone and departed. Reverend Balfour is an innocent man," said Dr. Bell, just as he left for our cabin.

"What does he mean?" I asked Stevenson.

"Dr. Bell must believe it is as if the Reverend Balfour is two people in one or that he has two personalities. The real Balfour is an innocent man. When Dr. Bell removed the tumor, he took away the religious maniac who killed the girl," Stevenson replied. "I would argue that he should not be held liable for the actions of his second, evil self."

Stevenson took a generous pull from the flask. "You know, it might be worth a story," he said, rather idly.

35

The Reverend Balfour moved an arm, and his eyes fluttered. I checked the pupils of his eyes. They were equal, and he breathed easier.

"You know better than me. If a small tumor can cause a mild-mannered man to become a murdering maniac, could a potion, some sort of witch's brew, do the same?" Stevenson asked.

I thought of my experience at the Hospital for Incurables. "Aye, the brain can react to disease, drugs, or injury in mysterious ways. If you someday return to Edinburgh, look up Dr. Jekyll in the chemistry department. He would certainly be able to provide more information."

Stevenson furiously scribbled in his notebook and offered the bottle. I had to keep my wits about me and refused. "Tell me more about Miss Yates."

He laughed. "You poor, poor sod. You're smitten. Her parents died last year from typhoid fever, leaving her and a young brother in deplorable circumstances. She is distantly related to the Balfours, so the minister took them in. The girl was supposed to be a nurse to the lad, but the wife makes her work like a scullery maid. When he became ill and left the church in Aberdeen, he found a position as a missionary to a tribe of Indians in the far west. He sent the lad to a foundling home and kept the girl to look after his son. I pity the poor heathens who must listen to his dogmatic rants."

I mulled over this tragic story until our patient stirred. He again moved his right arm, and both his eyes flickered for a moment. He uttered a long sigh and grasped my hand. There were more signs of slight, but encouraging, improvement as a new day dawned.

As I sat with him, I was having visions of sweeping Rebecca off her feet and taking her back to Scotland when, suddenly, she entered the sick bay holding a tray with a pot of tea and plate of eggs and bacon. She glanced at Stevenson, but rewarded me with a lovely sunny smile. "Arthur, I have been thinking of you. Poor man, are you famished and exhausted?" she asked.

Her hair was swept back and tied in a severe bun. She wore a drab grey gown, but, to my eyes, she was a vision of loveliness. Without another word, she poured tea and handed me the plate. "Enjoy the food. I must go back to Jimmy now."

She was gone before I could thank her, but, for the next few minutes, her words "I've been thinking of you" danced in my mind.

Then, a sad thought struck home. We were destined never to be together. We were both penniless. I had another year of school and more years before I could support a wife, much less her young brother.

A moment later, Bub entered and told me that Dr. Bell had paid him to look after the Reverend Balfour and I was free to go.

5 October, 1878

After an exhausted sleep I awoke to Stevenson's knock. We strolled a bit and took our usual place in the sun behind the ship's funnel. We had been chatting for a good hour or two when we heard a low moan that could have been wind sighing through the rigging or even a sea bird. Yet there was an immediacy to it that caught our ears.

When the moan became a scream, we leaped to our feet and followed the sound to behind a small deckhouse that served as a sail locker. It was there that we saw a huge sailor attempting to force Rebecca into the locker.

He had one hand to her throat and the other was ripping the front of her gown. We both leapt forward to rescue her. Stevenson reached the man first, but was batted away as if he were a common housefly.

I moved into the fray, but the big sailor loosened his grip on Rebecca and slammed his fist into my mid-section. The blow forced me to my knees, but afforded me a moment to watch the man.

His face was red with lust and rum. His nose was twisted from some long-lost battle. There was a gold hoop ring in one ear and a sheath knife at his belt. A green tattooed sea serpent twisted up one bare arm.

I regained my feet and jumped up as he aimed another blow. I had flailed away with boxing gloves at other students at the university, but this was not a gentlemen's match.

I narrowly avoided his punch, but, as he cocked back his arm for a killing blow, I remembered something I had learned from dissecting an arm in anatomy class: The ulnar nerve behind the elbow is extremely sensitive. With all my might, I aimed my clenched fist at his elbow, where I landed a terrific blow one inch above the medial epicondyle. He must have felt a horrible lightening-like pain because he roared and threw Rebecca in a heap on the deck.

Even though his right arm now hung uselessly at his side, he charged with his head down and reached for my neck with his good left hand.

I stepped to my right and barely avoided being pushed into the ocean. He had his knife half out of its sheath now, and if it had not been for his drunkenness, I would have surely been run through and killed on the spot. Instead, his knife sliced through the air a few inches from my ear.

I swung at his face, but he ducked, and my blow hit his shoulder. I heard the *snap* as his collarbone broke. Before either one of us could get in another blow, the third officer and three sailors subdued the brute.

I felt more than a twinge of jealousy when Stevenson got to Rebecca and whispered consoling phrases into her ear. He even covered her bare bosom with his seedy velvet coat. Stevenson was a ladies man, and I feared that he might try to take advantage of her distress.

I dashed over and wrapped my tweed coat around her shoulders. Instantly she stepped away from Stevenson and threw her arms around my neck, sobbing convulsively.

I held her close. She moved her head onto my shoulder. We clung together until her sobbing stopped. Holding her was such bliss, such pure sweetness.

"Oh Arthur, you were magnificent. I wish we could spend more time together, but I must get back and help the Balfours."

As we walked to the Balfours' cabin I asked about her life. She still clung tightly to my arm. "When my parents died, I vowed to earn money so I might study medicine in Edinburgh." She said this wistfully as if it were merely a dream.

"Oh, Rebecca, that is possible. The university allows women to study. Some professors don't believe women have the constitution to dissect a cadaver, but Dr. Bell is offering special anatomy classes to a few women. He believes women can be good doctors."

I did my best to comfort her, but she was still trembling when we arrived at the Balfours' cabin. Without another word, she again wiped her eyes, sighed deeply, and then entered the small second-class quarters. Immediately, I heard Mrs. Balfour accuse poor Rebecca of inviting the sailor's advances. "You have dishonored God and will never know the Lord Jesus!" I turned away with a heavy heart.

6 October, 1878

I attempted to pay Rebecca another visit today, but to no avail. Dr. Bell had sent the minister back to his room, so she nursed him day and night and suffered from the demanding brat, Jimmy, and his angry mother. I spent my time reading medical texts and writing last night's diary entry.

Today, after ten long days at sea, we ended our voyage. We docked at the Battery on the southernmost end of Manhattan Island. Stevenson was the first off the ship, hurrying to take a train across the continent. As he disappeared into the crowd, I wondered if I would ever see him again.

As we were packing, Bub brought a note from Rebecca. "Please, come to me, immediately, at the place where you usually meet Mr. Stevenson," it read.

She was leaning over the rail, staring at the water and the distant buildings. Worried that she might be about to leap overboard, I ran and took her hand.

"I thought I might never see you again," I said.

"I wanted to thank you for saving me from that brute before we parted forever."

"Forever? Is that Indian reservation so far that we shall never see one another again?"

"Arthur, please." She bent closer and touched my lips with her index finger. As I tried to kiss it, she pulled it away. "You must never tell a soul what I am about to tell you."

"I promise."

"The minister is not going to the Indians. That is just a story to fool people. Just before he became ill, he met an American who was traveling in Scotland. This man invited him to preach down South."

"Why would he invite a Scot to preach in America?"

At first, she did not say anything. For a long moment, we watched gulls making great swooping dives in the ship's wake to find tidbits of garbage in the salty water.

"I don't know all the details, but I have a sense that it has to do with a pro-slavery secret society. You see, the Reverend Balfour always preached that the Bible says Negro people are God's disobedient children, the cursed children of Ham, and therefore destined to be slaves to white men."

"But, that is ridiculous. I have read the Bible and I don't see how anyone could reach that conclusion."

"I don't know, but it all scares me. And he mentioned something about us meeting him in a big city on a big river in the middle of America."

"Wherever you end up, Miss Yates, please write and tell me."

"I shall, Mr. Doyle. Where will you be?"

"You can always address the letter to me care of the Rush Medical College."

For a moment I held her close and felt her heart fluttering like a small bird. She pulled away, and, without another word, ran off to the Balfours' stateroom.

Suddenly, I felt empty, forlorn, as if my life had come to a crashing halt. A minute earlier, the world had felt so warm and welcoming and full of promise. Now, it was a lonely, cruel place.

"Doyle, my lad, come. We have work to do." Dr. Bell called and insisted that I join him in visiting our patient. I was red-faced and clumsy in front of Rebecca, but managed to assist with the dressings. "Doyle, take care. Mind the antisepsis," said Dr. Bell. Reverend Balfour had no fever and Dr. Bell found no sign of inflammation in the wound. Our patient could speak, and, although weak, he had full use of his extremities. We learned that the family was to stay with the Reverend Henry Ward Beecher in Brooklyn prior to their trip to the Southland.

Dr. Bell insisted that once the Reverend Balfour settled down in America, he seek the services of a former Edinburgh physician to mind the antiseptic dressings. Balfour promised and we exited his stateroom.

I took one last longing look at Rebecca. There were tears in her eyes.

Back in our cabin, Bub folded and packed Dr. Bell's clothing. "Mr. Doyle, I want to ask a question," said he.

"Why of course, Bub."

"Sir, I can read and write, and I've studied lots of medical books. I wanna be a doctor for my people. Can I go with you, Dr. Bell and the other gentleman to Chicago as your personal valet? I can sure take care of your things, run errands, and keep your boots shined. And maybe you and the doctor put in a good word for me. Maybe you can help me get into Rush Medical School in Chicago."

I had never known a man of color. The occasional black man in Edinburgh seemed out of place and often menacing, but Bub was different. I liked him, and it would be good to have someone who knew the customs of America with us. I took the matter up with Dr. Bell.

Dr. Bell liked the idea, and we quickly struck a bargain. Bub became our valet and all-purpose assistant for his board, room, and ten dollars a week. I promised to teach him Latin medical terms and some anatomy.

"We can't keep calling you 'Bub.' What name was given to you at birth?" Dr. Bell queried.

"I once had the name of my master, but I ain't used it since I escaped and went up North. I'm scared of using that name because that man is liable to snatch me back."

"But, that's illegal since Mr. Lincoln signed the Emancipation Proclamation."

"Don't matter. My old master's a ghost, and the law don't apply to spirits. He claimed all his slaves are his property forever, no matter what paper Mr. Lincoln signed."

"No one is going to take you back to slavery . . . Out with it . . . You must have a name."

"Rufus 'Bubba' Freeman is what I be called now."

"I understand. But, before you got that name, what were you called?"

"Well . . ." He looked around nervously. "They used to call me Rufus Bedford Forrest."

"As in General Nathan Bedford Forrest?"

"Yes, sir."

I made a thrust with an imaginary sword. "The dispatches to the London papers carried stories about his exploits. He killed many a Union soldier with pistol and sword."

"The papers reported his death about two years ago, so you need not worry about him," said Dr. Bell.

A handcart was required for Rufus to carry Mr. Holmes' luggage from the ship to the dock, where he hailed a hansom cab, packed our things, and off we went up Broadway to the Metropolitan Hotel. We must have made a grand entrance, Dr. Bell in his well-tailored suit, Holmes, who had put away his deer-stalker cap for a black top hat and me, only slightly less sartorial in Dr. Bell's jacket. Rufus, still in his ship's uniform added to our distinguished group. At the mention of Angus Duncan, the desk clerk put us up in a fine suite of rooms and found a place for Rufus in the servants' quarters. By the time we were settled into our rooms it was time for dinner. For the first time, we had a meal together. Mr. Holmes made do with turtle soup and a small helping of vegetables but I tucked into a big porterhouse steak, oysters and a pint of ale.

7 October, 1878

Early this morning, Rufus proved his worth by guiding us through this strange, crowded, bustling city to the station just in time to catch the train that would take us across half a continent.

Our compartment had couches that the porter folded down at night and made up with fresh linen for sleeping. Rufus stowed our bags, but, as usual, I was in charge of the instrument case.

Dr. Bell settled in our compartment and returned to writing *A Manual of Surgery* and Holmes, as usual took up a German text on the chemicals derived from coal tar. Meanwhile, I explored the observation car, read my books, and searched the passing landscape in vain for some sign of Cooper's Mohicans or at least a Mohawk squaw.

I am sad to report that I did not see a single red man between New York City and Chicago. I had to be satisfied with the villages, cities, large fields of corn and wheat, and great herds of cattle that we whirled past. It was all so different from our wee country in the north of Britain. The dining car was as elaborate and the food was even better than on the *Devonia*, but I had little appetite.

Rebeccca's lovely tear-stained face haunted me wherever I turned. She was always in my dreams, on the pages of my books, and, once, the sight of a young red-haired girl made my heart leap. But, she was not Rebecca.

Rufus was a quick student. By the time we arrived in Chicago he understood the basic physiology and anatomy of the heart and lungs. I asked him about life as a slave, but he preferred to talk about his future in medicine. "I'm gonna set me up an office in Chicago and help all the poor folks who can't afford to go to a fancy white doctor. White. Colored. Chinamen. Indians. Don't matter. I'll give 'em all the best doctoring in the whole state of Illinois."

I scribbled these last notes just as Lake Michigan came into view. The rail line went through the dingiest part of Chicago, but Angus Duncan met us with his gilded grand carriage driven by a smartly uniformed footman. Mr. Duncan had indeed made a great fortune in America. His elegant fawn-colored trousers, dark brown waistcoat, and the heavy gold chain across his vest were signs of great wealth.

However, Dr. Bell bowed to no man, but greeted his fellow Scot and introduced me as his assistant.

Rufus sat with the Negro coachman in the driver's seat, and we were off through the streets of Chicago. I was dazzled by the new buildings that had been erected in the seven years since the Great Fire. We soon turned onto Prairie Avenue, an elegant tree-lined street with one great mansion after another that had most fortuitously escaped the flames which had devastated so much of this city. During the journey, Dr. Bell and Duncan jovially talked about old times. Holmes said nothing but observed Duncan with great intensity.

Duncan, like Dr. Bell, was a widower. Once we arrived at his three-story home, built of pink limestone and brick, a maid ushered us into a paneled living room. A lively fire crackled and blazed in a marble fireplace while we had tea and scones and little jam-filled delicacies that reminded me of home.

After tea the two men exchanged more stories about their school days, and Mr. Duncan talked about how he had built a great railroad empire in the West and South. Sherlock Holmes inserted himself into the conversation, rather abruptly. "Mr. Duncan, have any more of your employees met with sudden death?" The question hung in the air for several seconds. Mr. Duncan's face turned a deep crimson and he clutched his throat. "Angus, are you well?" Dr. Bell cried.

Mr. Duncan tossed off a half glass of malt whiskey and slowly recovered. "How, how did you know?" He asked.

"Simple, your letter indicated considerable anxiety and you used the words 'under attack'. The newspapers have made no mention of explosions or other direct assault, so you could only be referring to your employees, perhaps valuable, key employees," Holmes said.

"You are a canny one. Yes, two more of my most important men fell on the street, ceased breathing and were dead within minutes. The police have no clues." Angus said.

"In order to commence an enquiry, I suggest you put charts, maps and all material pertinent to your organization at my disposal," Holmes said.

It was an outrageous request but Duncan glanced at Bell. "I suggest you do as he asks," Dr. Bell said.

8 October, 1878

This morning, we went straight to the Chicago County Hospital. The morning clinic in the huge amphitheatre was attended by a few Rush professors and a handful of noisy students. It was only then that I realized American doctors greatly oppose Lister's new antiseptic method. Just as the clinic was about to begin, an angry student shouted, "No women! Get out!" The center of the commotion was a small elegantly dressed woman who beat her assailants back with an umbrella.

Dr. Bell raised his hand. "Behave like gentlemen or this clinic will be terminated. In Edinburgh, I welcome members of the fairer sex interested in the medical arts, and I shall do the same here . . . As should you."

The male students sullenly took their places. Bell offered his hand and escorted the woman to a place in the front row. She was a dark, sensual Mediterranean lass with twinkling grey eyes and black hair. The wrinkles about her eyes and lips did not detract from her beauty. The boys may not have liked women in their classes, but they ogled her attractive figure in a tight-fitting skirt and shirtwaist.

"Thank you, Professor. We, in America, admire your courage in teaching female medical students and your interest in the nursing profession. I am Emilie Droussard," she said.

When patients arrived and the clinic started, the students settled and were not so very different from my classmates in Edinburgh.

I took notes as the Rush students presented their cases. There was the usual run of patients with hemorrhoids, broken bones, and consumption, but nothing tested Dr. Bell's acumen until a student wheeled an impish little man of perhaps forty years into the small amphitheatre. He complained of a lump and pain on the right side of his abdomen. The Rush professors had diagnosed a tumor of the kidney.

The patient sat on the edge of his stretcher, dangled his legs, and grinned like a monkey. Dr. Bell looked at him, "Good morning, Mr. Ericsson. I see that you suffered an injury in the recent war."

The man proudly pointed at a scar just to left of center in his chest. "Yes, indeed, it was a Confederate ball. Special delivery on the first day at Shiloh."

"Your rib must have blocked the bullet from your heart."

The patient had a broad smile when he twisted around to show another scar on his back. "Oh no, sir. The ball went all the way through and festered. The surgeon drained a pint of pus and found the bullet." Mr. Ericsson then proudly removed a conical lead bullet from his trousers pocket. "Here it is."

Dr. Bell had the gleam in his eye that I had come to recognize when he was about to spring one of his great surprises.

"Would you be so kind as to stand up and drop your trousers?"

"Excuse me, Doctor. There is a lady present."

"Please. Indulge me, sir."

Ericsson blushed crimson, but dropped his pants.

"Gentlemen, normally the left testicle descends first and hangs lower. Please note that our patient's right testicle hangs lower than the left. This is a sign of *situs inversus*, a condition in which all organs are reversed. He survived the gunshot wound only because his heart is on his right side rather than the left. His spleen, normally on the left side of his abdomen, is the mass noted on his right." Dr. Bell sat back in his seat, folded his hands and cast an appreciative glance at the woman.

The Rush professor of surgery, Moses Gunn, who had made the diagnosis of a kidney tumor, scowled and rose to examine the patient. He first put his ear to the patient's chest and then minutely felt his abdomen. "Gentlemen, our distinguished guest, Doctor Bell, is correct. I bow to his diagnostic skill."

The students stamped their feet and clapped their hands. Amidst the uproar, a young man entered the amphitheatre and urgently spoke with Dr. Gunn, who then turned to Bell.

"One of our interns, Dr. Murphy, has a patient in the emergency room. Would you care to come along?"

"By all means," Dr. Bell replied.

The patient was a perfect specimen of manhood, certainly no more than twenty-five years old, muscular, and well-formed. Unfortunately, he was quite dead.

"It happened only a few minutes ago. A policeman was investigating a horse theft at a livery stable, and he observed the victim walking as normal as could be with a group of men. Then, suddenly, he said, 'Oh,' walked a pace or two more, stumbled, and fell to the ground," Dr. Murphy explained.

During Doctor Murphy's recital of the history, Dr. Bell minutely examined the body. "Were there signs of life when the policeman found him?"

"He was gasping for air and his eyes were wide open. It was as if he was pleading for help. That's why I rushed him to the hospital," the policeman, evidently an experienced detective, replied.

"Is this case similar to other recent deaths?"

"Why yes," The detective replied.

"Doyle, send for Holmes, immediately. Dr. Gunn, please arrange for an immediate post-mortem examination," Dr. Bell shouted.

I ran in to the street and hailed the first cab in sight. "A guinea for you. Straight to the home of Mr. Angus Duncan," I shouted.

"That will be two bits," the driver said.

"This gold guinea is worth ten times that amount. Hurry man, hurry."

When he saw the gold, he applied whip to horse and in no time I collected Holmes and returned to the hospital, post haste. We found our way to the hospital morgue, an ill-lit room in the basement, equipped with a rough wooden table, a tray of rusty instruments, and a bucket of water to sluice away blood. I kept my distance, but Holmes seemed to pounce on the body, sniffing, observing and touching the extraordinarily flaccid corpse. I could not help but notice the victim's open, staring eyes. It was as if he had watched his own death from some faraway place and had begged for mercy.

Dr. Gunn, with practiced ease, slit open the body from neck to belly and examined each organ in turn. There was nothing abnormal.

Dr. Bell and then Holmes sniffed at the contents of the stomach which held nothing more than partially digested bits of beef and bread. Holmes held his chin in one hand and closed his eyes for a long moment. Then to the policeman, he said, "Describe again, in as much detail as possible, your observations."

"It was as I said. The gentleman was walking as normal as any man with a group of friends. When he fell, his friends were immediately upon him, holding his hand and slapping his face. They would have removed his body if I had not found signs of life and insisted on taking him to the hospital."

"And did you observe anything unusual?"

"Not really, but it was a little strange that his friends did not go to the hospital. They abruptly left the scene."

"Did you notice anything else?"

"No, everything seemed perfectly normal . . . Although, there was a lady in black who seemed to be part of the group, but the moment the man fell to the ground, she rushed away."

Dr. Bell offered his hand. "Sir, you have uncommonly good powers of observation."

"Thank you, sir. It is part of our job," said the policeman.

There appeared to be nothing more to be seen, but Holmes gestured to the policeman. "One more thing, officer. Before you leave would you be so kind as to please turn the body over?" The policeman rolled the corpse onto its stomach.

"Aha, there it is." Holmes pointed to a speck of blood and a puncture wound on the man's left buttock. "This man may have been injected with curare, a deadly South American poison that causes near-instantaneous paralysis and death."

"Are you saying this was murder?" Dr. Gunn asked.

"Indeed, murder most foul."

"But, we must prove it. Doctor Bell will you kindly incise the area of the puncture," Holmes said.

"Doyle, my instruments, if you please . . ."

I opened the leather case, and, from the rows of gleaming surgical tools, Dr. Bell selected a straight scalpel, forceps, and two hooked retractors. He then, with great care, opened the puncture wound and dissected through the layers until he paused and murmured, "Doyle, hold the tissues apart with retractors."

I separated the skin and fat as he deepened the incision to a layer of muscle at the very end of the wound.

Holmes eyes never left Bell's flashing knife. "There in the depths of the wound, see, a few drops of the poison that were not absorbed after death occurred." Holmes said. He selected a glass syringe and drew up the whitish fluid.

"To prove the cause of death, I shall require a small animal. A rabbit or a cat would do nicely."

Within half an hour, two students returned with a sack that contained a writhing, spitting, clawing, grey rat. It was the size of a small cat and rather fearsome-looking. It took two students to hold the rat, a picture of violent activity with ears laid back, until Holmes drove the needle home injecting the deadly white fluid.

Instantly the rodent went limp and collapsed, but, curiously, he struggled to breathe for nearly ten minutes. During this time, his eyes were wide open, and I swear he seemed to be pleading with us to spare his life.

"There, gentlemen — all of the exact symptoms of curare poisoning. The man and the rat died from a lethal dose of this deadly poison used for generations by natives in South America."

That evening, Angus Duncan invited us to share a bottle of port. "Angus, Mr. Sherlock Holmes has proved your suspicion of foul play," said Dr. Bell.

"What? How?" Dr. Bell gestured to Holmes. "You can explain the matter better than I," he said.

"The man died after assailants injected him with a rare South American poison. The natives use this poison on arrows to kill animals. The poison is short lived and leaves no traces. We were fortunate to take a sample early. You must insist on a police investigation."

"The Chicago Police are more concerned with taking bribes than investigating crime, but I shall notify the Commissioner. Young man, I will pay handsomely if you can get to the bottom of this matter," Angus said.

10 November, 1878

Over the course of this last week, I have been busy. So busy that I have failed to record my thoughts in this journal. But, I shall fill in all the blanks of the past few days in these next few pages.

I assisted Dr. Bell as he repaired crooked legs, operated upon joints infected with tuberculosis, and repaired cleft lips. Rufus quickly learned how to clean instruments and swab down the skin of patients with carbolic solution. I have assisted at surgery, and Dr. John Murphy, the delightful, red-haired Irish intern, gave the anaesthetic for all our surgical cases.

At first, only Dr. Gunn and a few students were present, but, as news of Dr. Bell's incredible results with the antiseptic method became known, more and more students and physicians began attending his clinics.

Every single day, Emilie Droussard sat in the front row, avidly taking notes and occasionally asking questions. Dr. Bell seemed to take great delight in her attention. Additionally, by the end of the week even lay people were drawn to witness Dr. Bell's feats of surgical skill.

During the afternoons, Rufus and I had the run of Rush Medical College, which was just across the street from the hospital. Most of the students were rough, uneducated country laddies, but still good fellows. Sherlock Holmes spent his days with Angus Duncan, poring over files, lists of employees. At night, he prowled the city, searching for anyone with information.

Beyond the hospital and medical college, it seemed like every other establishment in the city was a saloon, gambling den or brothel. I had no money for gambling and was not interested in the offerings of the painted ladies, since I know too well the horrors of venereal disease. Even when tempted by a particularly attractive wench, the vision of Rebecca's lovely face always appeared to keep me from committing an unspeakable sin.

Tonight, after working all day, I invited Rufus to Peachey's Saloon, a good Irish pub that sells an honest mug of ale. A group of Rush Medical College students had congregated there to drink. In the center of a gang of students, an overgrown Wisconsin farm lad by the name of Carl Lindborg was telling stories, to roars of laughter. Over six feet tall, with massive arms and legs, he had a huge head of curly blonde hair, rosy cheeks, and a baby face. As he spoke, he held a lit El Perfecto in the side of his mouth and punctuated the best moments in his story with a wave of the cigar.

I tried to push my way inside the circle around Lindborg. "Excuse me. Pardon me," said I, but nobody budged. Did bringing Rufus make me an outcast?

Lindborg heard my Scottish accent. "I hear that a Scotsman knows how to drink," he barked.

"I was born in Scotland, but have some Irish and English blood, so I wouldn't exactly call myself a Scot. The name's Arthur Conan Doyle."

"Well, Artie . . ."

"The name is Arthur."

He pointed the El Perfecto Cigar. "Whatever you call yourself, my friend, might you be interested in challenging this wee American lad of Swedish descent to a chugging contest?"

"It would be my pleasure to teach you a lesson on how to drink, sir, but I believe it would be more fitting to propose an arm wrestling match instead."

"Even better. I have milked cows my whole life and never lost an arm wrestling match." As the other students laughed and snickered, suddenly the circle around him parted and I was ushered into the center.

Carl and I struggled and grunted and strained for a good minute or two before he bested me. Within five minutes we were smoking cigars together, and I could not help but like this giant of a lad who must not have been more than eighteen.

As Lindborg and I chatted, he continued to imbibe while I smoked deeply on one of his cigars. The discussion turned to the scarcity of bodies for anatomical dissection in Chicago. . "Artie, I have me an idea," Carl said.

"It is Arthur."

"Either way, follow me." He led me and a group of medical students to a uniformed copper sitting on a stool at the far end of the bar. The police officer was eating a late dinner of boiled eggs and a pig's foot.

Lindborg pushed a pint across the bar to the officer. "Paddy, my friend, would you care for a drink?"

"I would not turn down a pint," said the copper.

After Paddy had several mugs of good beer, as well as a dram or two, Lindborg patted his back. "Paddy, my dear old friend, may we borrow your wagon for a bit?"

The policeman nodded and we were off. Carl and his lads stopped at their lodgings to gather spades, shovels, a large canvas bag, a chisel, and a hammer. It appeared as if this were a common student activity. A half-dozen of us, including Rufus, piled into the four-wheeled wagon drawn by one poor horse.

We traveled through the darkened streets, mostly north and east by my calculations, until we were beyond the city limits. As we drew nearer to Lake Michigan a cold rain, driven by a northeast wind, sprung up. We plodded along until a large, decrepit sign announced "GRACELAND CEMETERY."

For a moment, I wondered if we were any better than MacLure, the Greyfriars Killer, but then I reasoned that what we were doing could save a good deal of lives. I proceeded along with Lindborg.

Inside this dreary place there appeared to be several acres of gravestones surrounded by a broken down fence. The wind sighing in rows of trees and the patches of fog lent a ghostly aura of gloom. I shivered with cold and had real misgivings about the whole enterprise. "Carl, we shouldn't be doing this."

"Look here, Artie. You can stand there and look down on me from your high and mighty Scottish pulpit, or you can roll up your sleeves and help. Either way, we are going to do this."

"CALL ME ARTHUR! And what if . . ."

"The other medical schools have the money to buy bodies, but, if we want to learn anatomy, it is up to us to provide the specimens. And so, what choice do we have?" said Carl.

Rufus stepped forward, "I'll stand here as your lookout. Mr. Doyle, why don't you stay with me?"

I paused, considered his proposal and sighed. "All right, then, Rufus and I shall be your lookouts."

Carl and his boys continued until they came to a fresh grave in the pauper's section. With the help of a shaded lantern, the boys set to work shoveling the loose wet dirt until their spades struck the wooden coffin.

I shivered in my bones at the hollow awful sound. It was one thing to dissect a body — an innate thing — beneath a bright light and quite another thing to bring up a fresh corpse from what was supposed to be its final resting place.

The combination of the sighing wind, the flickering lights, the brush of tree limbs, and the shadows playing amongst the statues and gravestones was more than enough to take away my thin veneer of rational scientific thought. Perhaps there really were spirits and ghosts that haunted places such as this.

Lindborg, with practiced ease, chiseled off the top of the coffin. The boys removed the body, placed it in the canvas bag, and carried it to the police wagon. The boys passed a bottle to me. I quickly got over my qualms and looked forward to testing my knowledge of anatomy against the Americans.

Within the hour, we returned the wagon to Paddy and the body was safely on the dissecting table in the anatomical laboratory. The corpse was that of a well-dressed, well-formed young man. He was clearly not a pauper. While we removed his clothing, the body was face down on the table. "My God, there is a puncture wound in his left buttock," I gasped.

We then turned the body face up and stepped back in horror. His neck had been slashed from ear to ear, leaving a gaping bloody wound.

It was then I noticed the open, desperate eyes that, though dull and dead, seemed to plead for mercy — just like the rat. There was also the unmistakable odor of carbolic acid about the man's neck.

Carl and the rest of our tipsy companions quickly sobered at the sight of that ghastly slashed throat and the eyes, dulled by death, but still wide open, pleading for an answer as to why he was murdered.

The other students faded away from the dissecting room leaving just me, Carl, and poor Rufus alone with that awful corpse. Before he came to Rush, Carl had been apprenticed to a busy surgeon and had seen his share of wounds and death, so he was not shocked.

He even had the presence of mind to lower the shades and darken the windows. "The murderer would not be happy to know that we have discovered his victim," said he.

At first I did not understand, and then it struck me. When Holmes had made his clever discovery of homicide, he had unwittingly thrust us all into danger. Yes, here was another dreadful murder. I couldn't make head nor tail of this case.

"Rufus, please fetch Mr. Holmes, immediately," I said.

11 November, 1878

In the wee hours of the morning, Holmes and Dr. Bell arrived, accompanied by Angus Duncan. Dr. Bell quietly inspected me and Carl and shook his head disapprovingly. "Doyle. Please remember, we are guests in this country. You must promise to refrain from engaging in unlawful activities," said he.

"Doctor Bell, sorry, sir, but —"

"Robbing graves is a criminal offence."

"Sir", I stammered, "It . . . It was only a prank and the students — they are doing it for the sake of their studies. They need anatomical material."

"Even in the name of medical research, it is still illegal."

"How did you know this cadaver was stolen?" I asked.

Dr. Bell smiled. "You look guilty. Perhaps Mr. Holmes can produce more evidence on a crime," he said.

"There was a ghost of a smile on Holmes' lips. "I have spent several days prowling the city. Graceland Cemetery has a fine stand of hazelnut trees and there is a hazelnut leaf stuck to the underside of your muddy left shoe."

His astounding observational skills once again amazed me. If only I could learn to observe, deduce, and make a correct diagnosis.

Holmes then circled the corpse, observing it with great intensity and sniffing its odors.

Mimicking the technique, I had seen Dr. Bell use in the past, I put my chin on my knuckles and studied the cadaver. The body was undressed, but the well-tailored suit of clothes we had removed suggested that he had been a gentleman. Even in death, the facial features were symmetrical, and the body was well-built. Aside from the puncture wound and slashed throat, there were no other outward signs of injury and nothing to indicate that the victim had attempted to defend himself.

"Roll the body over, and a probe, please," Sherlock Holmes requested.

Holmes held the iron probe delicately between his right thumb and forefinger. He pushed the instrument into the puncture wound at a slightly upward angle. The wound appeared to be two inches deep. By measurement, the corpse from the crown of the head to the heels was about five feet ten inches.

"The needle that delivered the poison was thrust from somewhat below the wound in an upward direction, suggesting that the assailant was shorter than the victim," Holmes surmised.

After he had minutely inspected the body Holmes turned to the slashed throat. The wound was cleanly incised as if the assailant had used an extraordinarily sharp instrument.

With steel hook retractors, Carl and I separated the edges of the wound. Holmes held a lamp close to the wound. Dr. Bell gasped. "This is no ordinary slashing. The killer was a gifted surgeon who dissected each layer with supreme precision and avoided the great arteries and veins."

We eagerly peered into the wound. "Great God in Heaven! There's no thyroid gland!" Holmes exclaimed.

Indeed, the thyroid gland, a reddish, paired organ shaped like half of a peach, was missing. It normally covered the trachea and the jugular veins, but in this case it was gone. The wind pipe and great veins were uncovered in the depths of the incision, and the vessels that had supplied blood to the gland were now neatly divided.

Mr. Duncan, who had silently held back away from the corpse, finally found his voice. "Who could have committed such a dreadful crime?"

"This was clearly the work of a devilish surgeon. Angus, we must notify the police at once," Dr. Bell said.

"The police have done nothing to investigate the previous cases and I fear they will do nothing about this. Instead, let me send for my good friend, Allan Pinkerton," said Duncan.

Every Scot knew of Pinkerton, a native of Glasgow who had founded a famous detective agency. He was a source of national pride because he had once saved Abraham Lincoln from assassination.

Pinkerton arrived in a carriage drawn by four fast horses just after dawn. He was stocky, with a high forehead and a bushy, black beard. He was accompanied by two detectives. After greeting us brusquely he examined the body in minute detail and then took a series of photographs. "Gentlemen," said he, "you are no longer needed. I shall take this case from here."

Duncan jovially clapped Dr. Bell on the shoulder, "That's enough for one evening. Gentlemen, it has been a long night. Let us all repair to the Tremont Hotel for breakfast."

We went off in two carriages. Rufus came along, but refused to enter the dining room. "I'll get me a bite in the kitchen," said he.

The sumptuous dining room, decorated in gold gilt, overlooked Lake Michigan. Carl Lindborg and I were out of place in our shabby clothing and dirty hands, but we took our place at the table and set to work on ham steak, fried eggs, and sweet rolls slathered in butter and jam. Holmes, in his usual abstemious way, toyed with eggs and a bit of ham.

When the party settled down to coffee and morning cigars, Allan Pinkerton tapped his glass for attention. "Gentlemen, to solve this case I need to know as much information as possible, so, at the request of Mr. Duncan, I have decided to hear from our medical colleague, Dr. Joseph Bell."

Dr. Bell, in his usual manner, laced his fingers together over his chest and spoke in his quiet, squeaky voice laced with a wee bit of a Scottish brogue. "We have two victims with similar puncture wounds. Mr. Sherlock Holmes, my associate, proved the presence of a poison that caused paralysis and death within a few minutes. The poison was undoubtedly South American curare. The second victim was rendered helpless by the same poison, and, either while still alive, or immediately after his death, the assailant removed the victim's thyroid gland."

I nearly choked on my cigar. Now, this Holmes fellow, as brilliant as he is has become Dr. Bell's associate. I felt rather left out.

"Hmm. Well . . . What, exactly, is the function of this gland?" Allan Pinkerton asked.

"We know very little. However, Swiss surgeons have observed a decline in all body functions, especially intelligence, after the removal of enlarged thyroid glands. The condition resembles cretinism that occurs in children born without a thyroid gland."

"What would be the purpose of removing the gland from an apparently healthy young man?" Angus Duncan asked.

"I have no answer for that. The Swiss have implanted various glands from animals into patients with declining sexual and mental function, but, thus far, their experiments have failed."

When a memory of a lecture by our chemistry professor flashed into my mind, I could not help but add my bit to the conversation. "Sir, at university back in Edinburgh, Professor Brown proposed a series of experiments using fresh extract of the thyroid gland to increase intelligence. Is it possible that this murder is part of such an experiment?"

Dr. Bell glanced my way with fresh interest. "Doyle, my lad, you may have hit upon a motive, but I believe it is still far too early for us to know for sure. What we do know is this. The perpetrator is undoubtedly a well-trained surgeon with a detailed knowledge of chemistry. His use of carbolic acid indicates that he wanted to keep the gland free from infection for some as-yet-unknown use."

I was across the table from Pinkerton and Bell, who were sitting together. The detective's expression went from concentration and interest to a rather condescending smile and annoyance. "Professor Bell, you and your assistants may thrive in the world of academia, but detective work is a bloody and dangerous game that provides little room for a bookish gent such as yourself. I thank you and now hope that you will stick to your ivory tower, and let me and my agency do what we are famous for."

A crimson blotch rose on Sherlock Holmes' cheeks. He stabbed the air with his long, delicate index finger. "Detective work need not be bloody and dangerous, but rather an exercise in observation and deduction. One person could not have poisoned the victims and carried off their bodies alone. There must have been a gang. And sir, don't you at least want to know how the poison was delivered?"

"Ah yes, you have a theory about that, as well, I presume."

"I do, indeed."

"Well, let's have it."

"A hollowed out walking stick, or, perhaps, an umbrella with a plunger connected to a retractable needle at the tip of the stick, could easily deliver the poison. A type of *sword cane*, if you will. The victim would be unaware of his assailant's approach until he felt the prick of the needle, and then it would be too late." As he spoke, Holmes jabbed Mr. Pinkerton in the back with his index finger.

Pinkerton jumped to his feet, "Touch me again, sir, and I shall break that finger of yours!"

"Sir, I was merely demonstrating the murderer's technique," Holmes replied

I had, during the conversation, been idly looking about the room and spotted a woman wearing a flowery hat. Her face was hidden by the hat and a newspaper. When Dr. Bell spoke she crumpled the paper, and I had a glimpse of her black curly hair and worried eyes. She looked like the woman who had attended Dr. Bell's clinics, but, before I could make out her features, she turned away and hurriedly left the dining room.

A tall, distinguished man with a droopy mustache and greying hair met her at the door. They paused long enough for me to see that he was wearing a grey suit with a decoration in his lapel. She carried an umbrella even though the day promised fair weather.

Refreshed by the meal and several cups of strong coffee, we left for the medical school with Angus Duncan. "Angus, I fear that Mr. Pinkerton cares little for our observations," Dr. Bell mused.

"He does things his own way. He and his agents have solved many crimes involving train robberies and counterfeiting; however, he is still smarting from his failure to capture the notorious James Gang."

The day's clinic began with the usual bustle of house officers (what the Americans termed "interns") and students, arriving to take their places in the theatre. There was more than the usual interest today because the patient was a young woman with a tumor on the side of her face. Several local surgeons had declared her beyond help.

To my surprise, for the first time, Holmes accompanied us to the operating room. Dr. Bell gave me a rather condescending glance. "For this operation, I have asked Mr. Holmes to assist because of his anatomical skill."

I scrubbed with greater care than usual, and Dr. Bell insisted that we wear a clean butcher's apron over our clothing. Unruly students were noisily shelling and munching on peanuts in the back row until Dr. Bell shot them a stony glance. He never tolerated nonsense from students — whether in Edinburgh or America. When he removed his frock coat and rolled up the sleeves of his white shirt, several older surgeons guffawed.

"Are you not afraid of soiling your white shirt?" one of the surgeons asked.

"Better to soil one's shirt than the wound," Dr. Bell answered.

The operation was long and intricate. At one delicate point, Bell seemed to tire and to my amazement, Holmes took up the knife and with great skill dissected the last bit of tumor without damaging the nerves that controlled facial expression. After he was done, and when the girl had awakened from the ether, Dr. Bell sighed and thanked Holmes. He then answered questions concerning the antiseptic method.

Emilie Droussard, as usual was in the front row. She lingered after the operation and approached Mr. Holmes. I overheard a bit of their conversation. She asked about his surgical training. As near as I could tell, Holmes said he had been an apprentice to a surgeon in London, but had left for Edinburgh to study antiseptic chemicals with Dr. Bell. Sherlock Holmes seemed quite charmed by the twinkle-eyed lady and in parting, bowed and held her hand for longer than socially required. It was the first time I had seen him take an interest in another person.

We were both dead-tired, but Carl was eager to dissect the cadaver. Several students had already opened the abdomen under the watchful eyes of Dr. Gunn, but the intestine had gone putrid and, despite wreaths of tobacco smoke, the smell was overpowering.

Several students were especially keen to dissect the intricate plexus of nerves in the neck that led to the arm. Rufus seemed oblivious to the smell and eagerly followed our work, asking questions all the while. Carl and I took turns poking and cutting into the body.

Sadly, muscles and nerves are never as clear as depicted in a book. We first stripped away the skin and then separated muscles and dissected beneath the clavicle.

I set out to display the origin of the median nerve with a great deal of confidence, but the scalpel and forceps soon became slippery with fat and, for a while, I was hopelessly lost. Together, Carl and I finally found the junction of the medial and lateral cords of the brachial plexus that formed the median nerve. It was then easy to trace the median nerve in its course next to the humerus bone.

The dissection had taken so long that most of the students had drifted away. It was early evening before we decided to have a beer and a bite to eat at Peachey's Saloon. Just as Rufus went off to visit his new friends at the Tremont Hotel, the dean of the medical school thrust a letter in my hand. The name, Rebecca Yates, was on the envelope, and my heart soared.

I wanted to tear open the envelope, but decided to wait until I could savor her words in the quiet of my room. Carl loitered to clean and put away his dissecting instruments while I left the building with my mind on Rebecca.

There was the sound of hurrying footsteps, and I was dimly aware of something moving in the periphery of my vision. But, when I halted, scanned the street, and listened, I did not see anything in the gathering darkness. I should have waited for Carl, but memories of Rebecca's kiss had overtaken my senses.

I paused in the midst of my fantasy. The street was suddenly silent, deadly silent. Why had I walked out alone?

In a moment of terror, I remembered the walking stick filled with poison and started to run.

Hands grabbed me. Sharp pain shot through my arms and back. It was not the sting of a needle. Ruffians wrenched my arms behind my back and forced me to the ground. I struggled until rough hands held a cloth soaked in chloroform over my face.

I fought against the sweet fumes. And from a great distance I heard a soft, melodic American-accented voice, "Take care. He will make a fine specimen."

12 November, 1878

Early this morning, I woke up and thanked God that I was still alive. I was in Carl Lindborg's bed. He was sleeping on the floor next to me. When he saw me trying to get out of bed he jumped up. "Artie, please –" said he.

"It is Arthur."

"Either way, don't get up too quickly. Just sit back and tell me what you remember."

Through a chloroform haze, I told him that I recalled bits and pieces of my attempted abduction — rough hands dragging me, my heels bumping on the cobblestones, flashes of light, someone screaming, fists flying, shouts, curses.

Carl half-carried, half-led me through the streets of Chicago to Angus Duncan's house and into his parlor. I was still groggy and had only partially regained my senses. Dr. Bell and several other gentlemen from Rush Medical College were having breakfast together when we arrived.

"Good heavens. What happened?" Angus asked.

I told them what I could of the moments before being overcome by the chloroform. Carl stepped in and told them how he had finished his work, and, fortunately, emerged from the dissecting room just in time to see two thugs drag me across the road to a four-horse carriage.

He screamed and tackled one of my assailants, but the other knocked him to his knees with a terrific blow to the back of the head from a stout, gilded cane. Carl went down screaming, "Help! Murder! Police!"

There were no police, but a group of medical students leaving Peachey's Saloon ran to our rescue and swarmed around the thugs. After an exchange of kicks and blows they dragged me from the carriage and pulled Carl back onto his feet. Then, the coachman whipped up the horses, the thugs jumped on, and the carriage rushed away from the scene.

Angus Duncan put down his china tea cup. "These days in Chicago, I have heard of more than one instance of thieves using chloroform on their victims," said he.

"However, these do not sound like common thieves, sir, for when was the last time you have heard of ruffians having a four-horse carriage?" Dr. Gunn interjected.

In his usual way, Dr. Bell asked a penetrating question. "Mr. Lindborg, please try to remember—and do be specific—did you see anything different or unusual about the carriage?"

Carl rubbed his forehead and thought for a moment. "It was very dark, but it seemed to be an uncommonly fine gold-leafed carriage with spirited horses."

"Did you hear anything?"

"The thugs cursed, and at least one student cried out when he was struck down. Amid it all, I do seem to remember a woman's voice from within the carriage."

A dim memory stirred. "Yes, I heard her say the words, *'Take care. He will make a fine specimen,'*" said I.

"Just before the coach drove away I also heard someone saying a general would be damn angry. It could have been a woman's voice. I'm not sure. If those goons hadn't attacked me from behind, I swear I could have taken them all." Carl added.

"Doctor Bell, Is this episode related to those two recent deaths and your theory of murder by poisoning?" Dr. Gunn asked.

Dr. Bell mused, "Well, one need not rush to any conclusions."

"You must have formed some opinion," Angus Duncan said.

"Ahem I cannot make a conclusion based on our current evidence. Mr. Holmes, what is your opinion?" Dr. Bell asked.

Holmes finished his usual cup of extra strong coffee before replying. "The term 'specimen' is an unusual one to be used in the context of a common robbery, but not unusual for use in a scientific experiment. For example, Doyle is similar in stature and age to the two recent victims. Angus, tell us, what were the physical characteristics of the first two victims?"

Angus pondered a moment. "By Jove, they were both well-built men, of about the same stature and age as young Doyle."

"Were autopsies performed?" Holmes asked.

"Relatives took charge of the bodies even as they lay on the street. There wasn't a funeral, as far as I can remember, because the men lived in a different city."

"Would it be difficult to exhume the bodies? I believe these murders are the work of a well-trained surgeon," Holmes said.

"I cannot believe that anyone in the medical profession would murder in cold blood for the purpose of removing an organ," Dr. Gunn replied.

"The case of Dr. Corcoran in Edinburgh, who paid for the bodies of recently murdered victims for anatomical dissection, was not so terribly different. He defended his actions by claiming that, since the victims were already dead, he could use them for teaching anatomy, thereby benefitting humanity," Dr. Bell said.

Dr. Isham, a professor of medicine at Rush, spoke for the first time. "That reminds me of Dr. Eli McGillicutty who grafted skin onto burn victims after the fire of '71."

"What ever happened to McGillicutty?" Dr. Bell asked.

"There was a great scandal when he experimented with grafting animal skin onto humans. All of his patients died. Some called it murder. He claimed it was to advance science, but county commissioners removed him from the hospital staff. McGillicutty has since disappeared," Dr. Isham replied.

The meeting broke up and the doctors went their separate ways. Doctor Bell was to present another clinic. "Doyle, my boy, you have had a difficult, perilous night," said Dr. Bell. "Take today off and rest until you feel up to snuff. Oh, and here is five dollars. You have more than earned it."

I was grateful for the chance to rest, but, even after several cups of hot tea and generous helpings of eggs and ham, I still felt awful and went to my room. I was too restless to sleep and tried to read my medical textbooks for an hour or two, but I could not get Dr. Eli McGillicutty out of my mind. He sounded exactly like the sort of physician who might experiment on human beings. The idea of human experimentation was deeply disturbing, especially when I considered that I had just narrowly escaped being the subject of just such an experiment.

But, then, we would not have anaesthetics, ether, and chloroform if doctors had not experimented on medical students and taken the drugs themselves.

I am venturing deeper and deeper into the heart of this mystery and this great, enigmatic American nation. I am filled with questions. Much of what I have always thought of as absolute in my life is beginning to shift and alter. What is right and what is wrong no longer seem as clear to me as they once did.

As I set down these events of the past few days, I realize we are embroiled in a complex mystery. Dr. Bell is in the dark, but the enigmatic Sherlock Holmes may well pierce the dark. With those confused thoughts, I drifted off to sleep.

13 November, 1878

Bright sun was streaming through the windows when I awoke. It was early in the morning and I must have slept a good ten hours but must have been dreaming about skin grafting for burns because the idea of it popped into my mind as soon as I was awake. Out of professional curiosity, I was determined to learn more about Dr. McGillicutty.

"Where can one find old newspaper stories?" I asked the cook during a grand breakfast in the kitchen.

"Ask at the Tribune downtown," she answered.

It was a cold day, but clear and brisk and good for a walk. I strolled north on Prairie Avenue with the railroad tracks and chuffing trains close by. Horse-drawn trams, hacks, and wagons of all description filled the bustling streets. Workmen were busily erecting new homes and buildings as high as six stories. A fellow on the street said they were planning one that would go up to eight stories and have a steam elevator. But, since Chicago is so flat there, were no interesting vistas, and my view of the lake was perpetually blocked by tall buildings.

My thoughts turned to my beloved Edinburgh. From almost any street in *Auld Reekie*, one may view a heathery shoulder of the Pentland Hills or glimpse a ship tacking down the Firth of Forth to the North Sea. Aye, perhaps I was homesick. It was just that the new buildings in Chicago did not have the character of our Parliament or St. Giles, and there was nothing so fine in all of Chicago as the statue of Charles II astride his charger.

Finally, I reached the Tribune building just off State Street. The lobby was grand, with brass railings and gas lights. I found a clerk wearing a green visor behind a desk. The worthless scamp ignored me for a good while. "Where I might find old copies of papers?" I asked.

"In the archives," said he.

"And where might the archives be?"

The smirking rascal ignored my question until I leaned over the desk and flexed a muscle. "Through that door, down to the basement. If you can't locate what you're looking for, ask for a drunken gent by the name of Fogarty," he finally answered.

I went down smooth, worn, stone stairs to the dingy basement. The sign on the door said "Archives." I proceeded through a dark corridor to a dim, musty room filled with stacks and stacks of newspapers and folders filled with clippings. I made my way through the jumble and came to a desk lit with a green oil lamp. Behind the desk was a gnome of a man with a small head of thick brown hair. He shuffled papers with hands as delicate as a child's.

I cleared my throat. "Are you Mr. Fogarty?"

"And, what in hell do you want?" was his reply.

"Information on a doctor by the name of McGillicutty."

"And who in the name of hell are you?"

"Doyle. I am a visiting medical student from University of Edinburgh."

The gnome cackled with laughter. "I might have known . . . Doyle, eh? Irish, are you?"

"My father is of Irish descent."

"And, I suppose you are a good Catholic."

"I was raised Catholic."

He cackled again, "And, now, you're a damn backslider. I suppose you take a drop now and then."

I did not respond.

The little man pulled a bottle from his desk drawer, took a generous swig and pushed the bottle across his littered desk. "Have a pull and then we shall see about Dr. McGillicutty."

"Thanks, but, no thanks." I wanted to keep clear head.

"More for me, then. Yes, I have information on every damn politician, businessman, and half the crooks in town. You can't tell one from another and, yes, there is a file on McGillicutty. I know that bastard well."

When Fogarty rose from his chair, he was less than five feet tall, but he quickly skipped through the stacks of newspapers and returned with a folder. His small stature reminded me of my mate Jimmie Barrie from university. Then, I remembered Dr. Bell's statement that the assailant in the poisoning cases was of small stature. "Have you had any medical training, sir?"

"Hell, no. Studied literature at Oberlin . . . Lot of good it did me."

"For a literary man, this must be a dismal place to work."

"Ach, you get used to it."

He cleared a space beneath the oil lamp and spread out a series of clippings and advertisements. The first story, dated November 1871, described Dr. McGillicutty's remarkable results in the treatment of burn victims. A brief biography listed him as an 1860 graduate of the Eclectic Scientific Medical School in Nashville, Tennessee, where he had won the prize for anatomical dissections. Next, he was a surgeon to the Confederate Army. In 1863, he had resigned from the Army to study in Paris and Vienna.

A photograph showed Dr. McGillicutty wearing a formal suit of clothes and a black silk hat. He had a thick black mustache. Gold-rimmed spectacles were perched on a thin, almost aristocratic nose. He appeared to be highly respectable and the sort of practitioner that one could trust with his life. He also appeared to be of short stature . . .

There was another article about his dismissal from the County Hospital. An advertisement, dated 1874, included a close-up photograph of his face and head without the hat. He was balding and his spectacles were perched lower on his nose. He still appeared to be a solid practitioner, but something was a bit askew about his eyes.

Dr. McGillicutty, in the advertisement, offered the highest quality drugs: cocaine, opium, quinine, digitalis, and extracts of all known plant remedies. The next advertisement was more interesting.

REJUVENATION THERAPY
DR. MCGILLICUTTY'S GLANDULAR EXTRACT
REVIVES SPIRITS, RESTORES YOUTH
&
INCREASES PASSION IN BOTH SEXES

When I saw the word "glandular" my heart skipped a beat. I hurriedly recorded the information in my notebook, drew a rough sketch of the doctor, and pushed the folder back to Fogarty. "Where is this Dr. McGillicutty now?"

"Ah ha, aren't you the nosey bugger? Any more intelligence will cost you a drink, sonny boy."

Fortunately, Dr. Bell had given me the five dollars, so I could afford a few drinks. His destination, Hinky Dink McKenna's Saloon, was several blocks away in a shabbier part of town. On the way there we passed several mansions where young men and well-dressed young ladies were coming and going. Piano music and feminine laughter filtered out through open doors even though it was the middle of the day.

"Are there always parties here?" I asked.

"Aye, this is Mother Brigit's." He paused for a moment and pointed to an especially gaudy mansion. "The finest sporting house in the world. You can hire a young virgin or an experienced older vixen to teach you the ways of the world. Take your pick."

Hinky Dink's Saloon was a big raucous tavern with a long mahogany bar, scratched wooden tables, sawdust on the floor, and dozens of men lifting a glass. We had no more than arrived at a spot on the bar next to the lunch counter when the barkeeper slid a double shot of whisky to Fogarty, who downed the liquor with one gulp. I had a beer, and we helped ourselves to free pickles and tasty roast beef sandwiches.

He showed no sign of intoxication, but, when he commenced talking about Dr. McGillicutty, he nearly shouted. "McGillicutty, the bastard, promised that if I took ten bottles of his medicine I would grow a half-foot taller and be able to please a woman all night long. The damn stuff didn't work, but he claimed he was brewing a new formula just for me."

Several men put down their drinks and cocked an ear in our direction. "Where is Dr. McGillicutty now?" I asked.

A crafty smile came over his face. "Well, ain't that a bit of a secret?"

"Please, I must know."

He looked at me for a moment and then relented. "I happen to know he has his own private hospital."

"Where?"

"It's in one of me files, somewhere in the archives. Come back tomorrow with a bit of cash and I'll have the address for you."

I reached for money to pay for our drinks and felt Rebecca's letter. How could I have forgotten?

I tossed some coins on the bar, ran into the street, and, with great care, slit open the envelope with my pen knife. I scanned the single page with her delicate writing and then read it through a half-dozen times.

Dear Mr. Doyle,

I must thank you again for your kind assistance and pray that this finds you in good health. The Reverend Balfour is regaining his strength and has had no more spells. We are staying with the Reverend Beecher, a very famous minister who was a good friend of President Lincoln. His sister wrote the story **Uncle Tom's Cabin.**

The Reverend Beecher is a strange man for being a minister, since he was involved in a scandal and was accused of seducing young women in his congregation. Of course, these malicious allegations are false. He is a kind man who treats me with great sympathy, almost fondness, but he has changed his opinion about slavery and now believes, like the Reverend Balfour, that the black people should not have been freed. Sadly, his health is failing, and I am not sure how much longer he will be of this world.

Now, I have exciting news. Since the Reverend Balfour is feeling better, next week we shall travel to Memphis. Perhaps we shall meet again there after all.

Sincerely Yours,

Rebecca Yates

There was not a word expressing any feelings for me. My world turned upside down. I folded the letter, tucked it my notebook, and turned back to the saloon. I wanted to get dead drunk, but the vivid image of my own father lying drunk on the floor crossed my mind. Shame and anger welled up in me. I refused to ever become like him.

Maybe I should just go to a sporting house and find out what it's really like to enjoy the pleasures of the flesh. But, Dr. Bell would not approve. Why should he? He is so different from me. Everything has been so easy for him. He comes from long line of medical aristocrats. His father was a third generation physician, while my father, a struggling artist, has never had a tuppence to his name.

However, it is also true that Dr. Bell lost his wife and his only son, yet he has never veered from his life's course. I lifted my shoulders and decided that I will NOT be deterred from a career in medicine by one small setback. I am done with feeling sorry for myself and with romantic yearnings. Miss Rebecca Yates can dally with her elderly minister all she wishes. I am through with her.

14 November, 1878

Immediately after Dr. Bell's morning clinic we went to the children's ward to select patients for surgery tomorrow. The young physician, John Murphy, pushing a dressing cart, led us on rounds, giving a brief history of each of the sick little patients.

Even though the hospital is relatively new, the ward was damp and chilly. Columns blocked light from dirty windows. Dr. Bell clucked at lazy slatterns who swept dirt into corners or under beds, but he tousled the hair and joked with small lads and complimented the girls.

Boys and girls were not separated on the ward, and most beds had at least two small occupants. Apparently there was little interest in children or their diseases because, aside from Dr. Murphy, Carl Lindborg and Rufus, there was only one physician present on the floor.

More than once, Dr. Bell raised his eyebrows. "This poor child needs fresh air, sunshine, and good clean milk," he said. Yet these items seemed to be in short supply. At least half of the children suffered from tuberculosis of the bone or lymph glands, and the rest had broken bones from being kicked by a horse or run over by an omnibus.

For surgery the next day, the professor selected a child with tuberculosis of the spine and a large abscess, and another whose chest was filled with fluid, collapsing the lung. I knew he would save both lives.

My feelings about Bell keep shifting. In Edinburgh, he seemed to take pleasure in ridiculing me now I see that his hard veneer is coat of armor to protect a sensitive disposition. Do all physicians have to harden their hides to survive? I wonder if I can develop the necessary toughness to carry on as a doctor . . .

Near the middle of the ward, we came upon a girl of perhaps three years of age who was breathing with terrible difficulty. Her little chest caved in each time she attempted to draw in air, and her lips and fingernails were dusky blue.

"This little one is suffering with the croup," said Dr. Murphy, just as the child gave up her struggle and stopped breathing.

Dr. Bell fixed his eyes on the dying child. "Her vocal cords are completely obstructed. Mr. Doyle, my straight bistoury, please."

I desperately looked at Rufus. I thought he had brought the instruments. He had assumed that I had them. I could barely get the words out. "I'm sorry sir; the instrument case must be in the clinic."

Bell's voice was filled with venom. "You left the instruments?!"

"Aye sir. I'm terribly sorry."

"Find me some carbolic acid, PLEASE!"

I sprinted through the ward until I found a vial of carbolic and then ran back to Dr. Bell with it. Without another word, he removed a small silver pocket knife from his vest pocket and cleaned it with the carbolic. Then, with no hesitation, he held the child's chin back with one hand and, with the other, sliced an incision down the middle of her neck. Black sticky blood oozed from the wound. With another stroke, he cut into the child's windpipe and twisted the blade to separate the tracheal cartilages.

Dr. Murphy stepped forward and mopped a glob of mucous away with a bit of gauze. The child's chest heaved. She took in a lungful of air through the opening and coughed out plugs of mucous. Her breathing settled down, and, like a miracle, color came back to her cheeks. Murphy ran to obtain a proper tracheotomy tube.

Dr. Bell rarely became angry, but, in this instance, he was steaming. He cuffed my shoulder with an open hand. "Mr. Doyle, at the very least I expect my clerks to be dependable. This child might have died because of your negligence!"

I left to fetch the instrument case. By the time I returned, he had settled down and was discussing the treatment of esotropia (the condition of being cross-eyed) with Dr. Murphy and the physician who had tagged along. I had some interest in eye diseases and listened intently, then thought of the spectacles perched on the nose of Dr. Eli McGillicutty and the slightly off-center appearance of his eyes.

After we had finished the rounds I screwed up my courage to speak. "Sir, I may have information on the murder cases."

"Doyle, I would prefer that you concentrate on assisting me only in the care of medical patients. Please, do not let your concern about crime interfere with your medical duties. Mr. Duncan is having second thoughts about my involvement in this crime. I shall be having lunch with him and Mr. Holmes, shortly."

Bloody hell, Sherlock Holmes will get the glory if he solves the case but I was determined to find the wretches who had attempted to kidnap me and learn more about skin grafting.

I saw the doctor off in a cab to his lunch. With great trepidation, I turned the damned instrument case over to Rufus with strict instructions for him to immediately go to Mr. Duncan's home.

The horse drawing the omnibus was spavined and limped on its hind leg. The driver used his whip, but it was not until mid-afternoon that I arrived at the Chicago Tribune building. I immediately went to the basement archives only to find Fogarty asleep in his chair behind his desk. I cleared my throat. "Mr. Fogarty . . . It is I, Doyle. We have an appointment," I announced.

He opened his eyes and gave me a bleary look. "Doyle? I don't know any Doyle. Who the hell are you?"

"Sir, you promised to give me information on the whereabouts of Dr. Eli McGillicutty if I returned today with some cash."

"Are you a damned spy — a damned bloody Pinkerton?"

"No sir. I am Dr. Joseph Bell's medical clerk."

"Oh, you are with Ding Dong Bell." His witticism sent him into cackles of laughter and he seemed to wake up. "That mad Scottish quack."

"Please, you were to tell me about Dr. Eli McGillicutty's whereabouts?"

"You should ask the Colonel down South in the red house. I don't remember…"

"Mr. Fogarty, does this help you remember?" I held out a two-dollar gold piece. His eyes cleared, and he opened a drawer filled with empty bottles. "Damn, I can't think without some whisky. If you want me to find McGillicutty's damn bloody file, go around the corner and fetch me a bottle."

I purchased a pint of Old Crown and hurried back. I could not have been gone more than half an hour, but, when I returned, the archives section was pitch dark. I struck a wooden lucifer friction match against the brick wall and made my way, step by careful step, through the corridor.

When the friction match spluttered out, I bumped into Fogarty's desk. I lit another match, and, in the flickering yellow light, I saw Fogarty sleeping with his head down on his desk. The oil lamp had been knocked over.

I lifted the lamp out of a pool of what looked like oil and then realized there was dark blood all over the desk. I dropped the whisky bottle and touched Fogarty's neck. He was not asleep, but, quite . . . dead.

Something protruded from his mouth. "Holy God!" I uttered, and stepped back from the desk just as the lucifer match burned my fingers and flickered out.

I stumbled my way back up the corridor and into the front office of the paper. "Murder! There's been a murder!" I hollered at the top of my lungs.

The next minutes passed in terrible confusion. One of the clerks went into the archives with a lantern, returned immediately, and vomited on the floor. In the chaos that followed, there were screams for police. "Notify Mr. Medill!" someone yelled.

Within minutes, two constables arrived on the scene. After being equipped with lanterns they went into the basement. I followed and beheld an awful spectacle. Fogarty's chin rested on the edge of the desk and a long knife protruded from his mouth.

Lamp oil and blood soaked the papers on the desk. One constable reached for the knife. "Don't touch anything," I warned.

The constables, more accustomed to dealing with vagrants and drunks than murder, readily agreed, and we returned to the first floor. The clerk, who yesterday had directed me to the archives, pointed in my direction. "There, that man. He is the murderer!"

The constables drew their revolvers and pinioned me against a large marble column, pulling my arms back and applying handcuffs. I was the victim of rough frontier justice — tried, sentenced, and executed by the mob before I had a chance to prove my innocence.

Fortunately for my health and longevity, a distinguished bearded gentleman, dressed entirely in black and wearing a silk top hat, had entered the room and quickly restored order. Much to my surprise, he was accompanied by Angus Duncan, Holmes and Dr. Bell.

Mr. Joseph Medill was the owner and publisher of the Tribune and had been the Mayor of Chicago after the Great Fire. He and my friends were having a long lunch at the Union League Club when he was summoned.

The constables described the scene in the basement, but their English was rather poor and the powers of observation were even poorer. "Fetch Allan Pinkerton," Medill ordered, after listening a moment.

Then, Mr. Duncan asked that I be released. Dr. Bell drew me aside. "Doyle, what in God's good name is the meaning of this?" he whispered.

I quickly explained my interest in Dr. McGillicutty and locating the newspaper file. "The murdered man is in the basement," I said.

Mr. Medill, sweeping his cane from side to side, quickly cleared the room. "I should've fired the damned Irish drunkard long ago! And the damn Democrats had a hand in this, I will wager."

Medill was still ranting when Allan Pinkerton arrived. "Who found the body?" he demanded. I stepped forward.

"Lead the way," he commanded.

During the hour or so since I had found the body, blood had congealed on the desk, but nothing else had changed. Mr. Pinkerton was about to remove the murder weapon. "May I examine the body?" Sherlock Holmes asked.

Pinkerton's face turned crimson with rage. "Damn, I will brook no interference," he said.

"I disagree. Mr. Holmes has forensic skills," Dr. Bell said. Holmes shoved Pinkerton aside and wrapped a handkerchief about the hilt of the knife. He gently moved it back and forth; the head moved with the blade indicating that it was solidly imbedded.

"The murder weapon entered slightly from the left of his mouth, went through the back of the throat, and is imbedded in the vertebra. From the volume of blood, I would wager that the tip of the blade severed the right vertebral artery. He may have temporarily recovered from the initial shock of the blow, only to die when he strangled on his own blood," Holmes said.

I held the grisly head while Holmes with considerable strength removed the knife. The letters C.S.A. were stamped on the blade. It was a bayonet.

"Have not seen one of these since the war," said Pinkerton.

"What does it stand for?" I asked.

"Confederate States of America." Mr. Pinkerton wrapped the bayonet in an old newspaper. "This may have been suicide, but I will investigate further." He glared at Holmes. "You, sir, had best return to England." With that, he stormed out of the cellar.

Holmes, however had not finished. "Look at this," said he.

Fogarty had scrawled something in his own blood on the desk top. The Gallic words *cinnte faoi ghlas* were nearly illegible but clear enough for Holmes.

"Doyle, return to the hospital and see to the little girl with the croup. Be certain, the intern is wiping away the secretions." I left him and Holmes poring over the crime scene and found a cab drawn by a spavined mare and driven by a half-drunk cabby. The girl was coughing and struggling for air because, as Bell, somehow knew, her trachea was filled with thick pus. I devised a suction syringe, attached to a rubber tube and sucked out the secretions. She breathed easier and took some broth. For me, it was a medical triumph. When Dr. Murphy arrived to take over her care just before midnight, she was peacefully asleep. Maybe, just maybe, I might become a tolerable physician.

When I returned to our lodgings, to my surprise Dr. Bell and Holmes were poring over notes before a blazing fire. "The little girl is much better," I said.

"Splendid, we have done some good on our trip. I must return to my practice after the next clinic, but you and Holmes will stay and assist Mr. Duncan in solving these crimes," Dr. Bell said.

He poured out a dram of sherry for me and motioned to a chair. "Please tell me everything that happened between you and this man Fogarty."

I started from the beginning and told him everything, from the time the thugs accosted me outside of the anatomy lab to my conversations with Fogarty. I showed him the sketches I had made of

Dr. McGillicutty. Doctor Bell grunted his approval and leaned back in his chair with his right fist under his chin. He tapped the sketch of McGillicutty. "Pinkerton suspects this man has connections to the foreign socialists who are intent on destroying Mr. Duncan's railroads by murdering his employees. He may be our man."

"But, only the first two victims were employed by Mr. Duncan," said I.

"That's true, but we don't know anything about the most recent victims. Now, tell me in more detail anything that you have not mentioned about the events of today."

"Well, Fogarty seemed to hate the Pinkertons and he said something strange along the lines of, 'Ask the Colonel down South in the red house.' I could make nothing of it. But, I do believe the words he wrote in his own blood are Gaelic."

I passed the page of my notebook with the words *cinnte faoi ghlas.*

"Aye, indeed. One would tend to think that he would write in his native tongue during his last moments. I shall have a chat with Mrs. O'Flynn as to their meaning."

At the mention of the cook's name I wondered what delicacies might be in the kitchen. I had missed dinner again. She had promised roast duck with orange sauce, but, due to the awful events that I had been involved in on this day, I ended up going to bed hungry.

And now, I cannot sleep . . .

So here I am, writing this entry to try to get my mind off my growling stomach. I came on this little adventure to see America, but I never dreamed that my life would almost be snuffed out by thugs or that I would be involved in solving a series of murders! Maybe I am not cut out for a life of adventure, after all.

15 November, 1878

I awoke this morning, hungry as a bear, with no thoughts at all about my grim musings of the past night. After a huge breakfast, I dashed off to the hospital. To my surprise, Holmes, who usually spent the morning in his dressing gown, reading books was in the front row, next to the woman, Droussard. The clinic was to be a post mortem examination of none other than Fogarty. Word had gotten around the medical community. The room was filled with doctors.

The diener rolled the corpse, covered with a sheet, into the amphitheatre while Bell arranged his instruments. The audience was silent when Bell drew back the covering and revealed Fogarty's body, which was the size of a small, hairless lad with undeveloped genitalia. Fogarty's lips were drawn back in a rictus of terror and his eyes were wide open.

"Gentlemen, you will agree that we have a most unusual case. This man, nearly forty years of age, has a body which has not developed beyond childhood. Our task is to determine the cause of this condition."

Bell made an incision from the neck to the pubis and quickly dissected the organs, which he placed in a pan beside the body. The heart, lungs, and stomach were perfectly normal, but the liver was in the advanced stages of alcoholic cirrhosis.

He then carefully placed the testicles, adrenal gland, and the thyroid in the pan and pointed to each with the tip of his knife. "Observe, these glands, the ones that we believe regulate the body — are atrophic."

Bell turned his attention to the gruesome head with the open mouth and congealed blood on the lips and gums. "Now, we will see a most rare abnormality of the pituitary gland."

He rolled the head from side to side. "What have we here?" He pulled the hair aside and demonstrated a smear of blood around a small hole in the back of the head. "It is a puncture wound."

He then drew his long, razor-sharp knife across the back of the head, from ear to ear and rolled the scalp back over the forehead, so that, when replaced, the face would appear to be untouched. Whatever instrument had made the puncture wound had penetrated deeply into the skull. "Mr. Holmes and Mr. Doyle, I need your assistance, please." With the tip of his knife, he removed a small fragment of metal imbedded in the skull. "Take this and keep quiet," he whispered in my ear.

I palmed the bit of metal, turned my back to the crowd, and slipped it inside my billfold.

"Mr. Holmes, will you kindly open the skull?" Bell asked.

Holmes took up the bone saw and cut the circumference of the skull and removed the skull cap, revealing the glistening brain with its convolutions, sulci, and veins. The physicians and students in the audience leaned forward with rapt attention. Perhaps some of them had never seen a human brain before.

Emilie Droussard's delicate features were deathly pale. I was surprised because she had witnessed operations and organ removal with equanimity, and I did not expect her to appear affected.

Bell lectured, while Holmes removed the brain, and, with infinite care, exposed the sella turcica, where the pituitary gland normally resides. Holmes with his superior knowledge knew exactly what to look for. "As anticipated, the pituitary gland, the supreme regulator of the body, has failed to develop. This undoubtedly caused Mr. Fogarty's small stature," Dr. Bell said.

When the crowd moved in closer to Fogarty's body, Emilie Droussard quietly left. Out of curiosity, I followed her out to the street.

She was adjusting her shawl, not far away, when a stooped, sallow-faced fellow came up to me. "You are one of the doctors caring for my little girl in the children's ward. I can't thank you enough."

"You should thank Dr. Bell. He was the one who saved her life."

The man poked his head close to mine. "I was in Hinky Dink's Saloon when I overheard your conversation with Fogarty. Since you helped my little Gracie, I kin tell ya this. If you want Dr. McGillicutty, there he goes." He pointed at a man walking in the opposite direction down the street.

Damn, McGillicutty had been in the audience all along. The man was stooped, had a bad limp, and his hat was pulled well down over his eyes. No wonder I had not recognized him in the audience. He was climbing into a hack less than a block away.

"No need to run after him. He lives at the Marshall Hotel at State and Van Buren." My sallow-faced friend spoke from the corner of his mouth. He scuttled away before I could thank him.

I wanted to hear Dr. Bell's last lecture, and it would not hurt to delay my meeting with Dr. McGillicutty. I returned and watched while Dr. Murphy neatly sewed up the incisions in poor Fogarty and Dr. Bell lectured on glands. He is as knowledgeable on the subject as anyone in the world, but very little is really known about them.

16 November, 1878

This morning, we saw Dr. Bell off on the morning train to New York. "We have not finished our task her, but you, Holmes and Doyle, must continue," he said.

I was determined to follow up my hunch about McGillicutty. Dusk came early, and the day was overcast, as in Edinburgh at this time of the year. The Harrison Street Omnibus took me to State Street which was only a short walk to Van Buren.

The streets were filled with disreputable men, poorly dressed women, and raggedy lads. Many carried unlit torches, and there was an air of excitement in the crowd. I hurried on, ignoring the moving swarm of people, and kept a hand on my wallet. The Marshall Hotel was a hastily slapped-together structure next to a gambling parlor and across the street from an empty lot filled with rubbish.

I shivered against the wind, and a knot of cold fear clutched the center of my chest. I started to freeze and then stopped myself. What was I doing? Did I have the nerve to do this? Was it foolhardy to pursue a criminal alone? Was I merely trying to prove my worth to myself and Dr. Bell?

I hesitated, but pressed forward into the shabby, dark lobby where a clerk directed me to the corner room overlooking State Street. "Who is there?" The gruff question came in answer to my knock on the door.

"My name is Doyle, assistant to Dr. Joseph Bell."

"The door is open. Enter." The voice had a strange tone, but was not unpleasant.

I entered the shabby room and immediately I backed away — repulsed by the overpowering odor of decay — and covered my face with a handkerchief. By the light of a single candle stuck in an old wine bottle I made out a bed, table, and a chair. Then, as my eyes adjusted, I saw movement under a pile of blankets on the bed. The dim figure gradually sat up and swung his legs off the side of the bed.

"Mr. Doyle, you have been looking for me?"

The voice had a peculiar resonance, and, as the figure gradually came into the candle's light, I saw a face disfigured by deep crevices, flat red patches, and a sunken nose. It was nothing like the photograph of Dr. McGillicutty. Was this an imposter to throw me off the scent? Maybe he had syphilis.

"Um, are you . . . Are you Doctor McGillicutty?" I stammered.

"None other."

"But, you don't look like your pictures."

"Mr. Doyle, you have followed me from the hospital, aye? I was there and saw you. I had to witness the post-mortem examination of poor Fogarty. He was one of my patients, you know?"

I took a step forward, but he held up his hand and motioned for me to come no closer. The hand was misshapen and the tips of the fingers ulcerated.

"Have they taught you about leprosy at Edinburgh?"

I recoiled in panic. "There might have been a lecture, but I don't remember."

His laugh was hollow and mournful. "Study my face and hands."

"But, I thought leprosy was only in the tropics."

"You are seeing the revenge of a monkey. I caught the disease from an experimental animal."

"What sort of experiments?"

"I worked on glandular extracts, looking for a cure for poor unfortunates like Fogarty."

"Then, you are the one. You murder men for their thyroid glands."

"No, no, no... Please, look at these hands. I have not operated for a long while." He waved his misshapen hands for me to inspect, although from a distance. I realized he was right. There was no way he could have performed delicate surgery with such deformed digits.

"But, you know about glandular extracts and —"

"Yes. My experiments with monkeys demonstrated that extracts of fresh tissue reversed the effects of total thyroidectomy. Sadly, I had to work on live, awake animals because, otherwise, anaesthetics reduced the potency of the glandular extracts I needed."

"And you used curare to prevent the animals from moving while you were experimenting on them?"

"Exactly. Until, one day, I administered too low a dose of curare to a poor creature. The monkey awoke in mid-operation and bit me. The damn animal infected me with leprosy."

"Sir, I believe that someone knows of your work and is killing humans to obtain the thyroid."

"You are correct. I suspect it is one of my former associates. Doyle, if you can stand the sight of my poor broken body, I would be willing to share all I know with you."

"Yes, Doctor, should we talk here or . . ."

"I haven't had a morsel of food all day. Let's go out and get something to eat. You know, your mentor, Dr. Bell may be the only surgeon in the world who can truly understand my work."

My heart went out to the wretched man. I wondered what it was like to have a horrible, incurable disease and feel death hovering over you. I shivered again and felt a premonition of ominous things to come.

The poor man pulled on gloves and turned the brim of his hat down over his face. Together, we exited his tiny room. As we made our way down the street to his favorite restaurant I made out a band of armed men lurking in the area just past the hotel. As if in a bad dream, I watched as they raised their weapons and took aim. *Dear*

God. Is this the end? I dove into the shadows just as shots rang out. I was unscathed. Dr. McGillicutty was not so lucky. A fusillade of bullets struck him down.

Instinctively, I crawled to his aid, barely avoiding injury myself when a slug tore through the sleeve of my heavy coat. McGillicutty had bloody holes in his chest. The sound of gunfire was suddenly drowned out by shouts and the clip-clop of horses on the pavement.

Was it a diversion to mask the murder? The night was lit by hundreds of blazing torches carried by demonstrators shouting for justice and higher wages. I huddled with McGillicutty on the sidewalk as a phalanx of mounted men dressed in white hoods and robes marched by, followed lads shouting and carrying banners denouncing capitalism. All of them were oblivious to poor Dr. McGillicutty.

I held two fingers against Dr. McGillicutty's neck. There was no pulse. He was beyond help. I escaped the raucous hubbub through an alley and crept between buildings until I was in the clear. There were no followers, but I was lost. It took several hours of wondering around until I came to a street I recognized and made it back to Mr. Duncan's mansion.

17 November, 1878

I slept late and after eggs and bacon in the kitchen, I reviewed these notes and lazily thought about home and school. In late afternoon a half a dozen carriages drove into the driveway. Well-dressed men, colleagues of Mr. Duncan, I supposed filed in to the great living room. From a nearby alcove, I listened to their agitated conversation. "They rioted last night, broke windows, killed a man, union agitators," one said.

"I attribute it to all those bastard foreign anarchists."

"Yes, and don't forget the damn socialists and the Klan."

I recognized the voice of Allan Pinkerton. "Gentlemen, my men will put down this riot and shoot the instigators."

"That's all well and good, but what is the Klan doing in Chicago?" another voice asked.

Pinkerton's voice rose. "Gentlemen, please, let me finish. There appears to be a group of Southerners who are attempting to ally themselves with union organizers to disrupt our nation."

There was a stunned silence. "How, in the name of God could that happen?" asked a gentleman with a fevered voice.

Pinkerton went on. "Gentlemen, yesterday a Gatling gun and a thousand new Winchester repeating rifles were stolen from the armory. I fear that they will be used to arm troops in the South or to foment uprisings among disgruntled workingmen right here in this fair city."

When they settled in to drinks and other matters, I crept up the stairs and found the door to Holmes' room open. "Doyle, please join me and close the door," he said.

The room was wreathed in clouds of Egyptian tobacco smoke, and Holmes was at his ease, reclining on a couch. "Arthur, we must compare notes. Now that Dr. Bell has left us, we must continue the investigation."

It was the first time he had used my first name. I warmed to the man. "How shall we proceed?" I asked.

"First, we know the men were murdered with the South American poison and second, the exhumed corpse had been operated upon and presumably killed by a skilled surgeon. Fogarty was evidently killed by an ex-Confederate soldier to silence him. Now, tell me about this Dr. McGillicutty."

I recounted my encounter with Dr. McGillicutty while Holmes sat with his fingers laced over his chest, looking into the flames. When I came to the part about the doctor's leprosy, he shook his head. "Sad, so sad."

When I finished he got up and paced back and forth, with that peculiar glint in his eye that often indicated deep thought. Your meddling may have caused that poor man's death but I suspect he was marked for murder anyway. Who knew you were meeting with him?"

"The father of the little girl with croup knew I wanted to meet Dr. McGillicutty. He seemed to be an honest workingman and had overheard my conversation with Fogarty in the saloon."

"Who else?"

"The Droussard woman left the post-mortem early and may have overheard my conversation with the girl's father."

"Ah, yes I spoke with her. She is an attractive woman. What were McGillicutty's exact words? Are you certain he said comrades instead of colleagues or classmates?"

Holmes continued pacing while I collected my thoughts. "I think he said comrade. What difference does it make?"

"The word colleague refers to a close associate, such as a physician's partner. The word comrade, on the other hand, is often applied to one's friends in a military outfit."

"That reminds me." I hastily consulted my notes. "Dr. McGillicutty was a surgeon in the Confederate Army."

"Exactly, and a Confederate bayonet killed Fogarty . . . Yet I cannot connect his statement about going south and a red house with anything concrete related to these murders."

"What about those three words scrawled in blood by Fogarty? Did you discover their meaning?"

"Mrs. O'Flynn confirmed that *cinnte faoi ghlas is* Gaelic and means 'sure lock'," I said.

"Strange, Sure lock, so similar to my first name, but it must refer to a type of lock box or a safe," he said.

There was a gentle knock.

"Who is there?" Holmes asked.

"Rufus."

"Come in, please."

Rufus stumbled into the room and stood before us, speechless. He trembled and twisted his cap in his hands.

"Rufus, snap out of it, man. What the devil is wrong?" I asked.

"They's coming after all us freedmen. To make us slaves again. I gots to go back to the *Devonia*. Get clear out of this country."

"Mr. Freeman, please calm down. Have a drink to settle your nerves."

Holmes filled a crystal glass with Port wine. Rufus gulped it down in one swallow.

"President Lincoln freed the slaves and the Thirteenth Amendment assured their freedom. You have nothing to worry about," said Holmes.

"They killed poor Mr. Lincoln and those ghosts marchin' in the street gonna tear up that 'mancipation proclamation. My lady friend's a housekeeper at the hotel and she told me that she was brushin' a man's suit when she seen them ghost clothes."

"Ghost clothes?"

"Yes sir. White hoods, long white robes. He had a set in the closet just like they was wearing on the street."

"Who is this man?"

"Captain Andrew Spencer. He was in the rebel army and rode with General Forrest. He got his right hand blowed off at the battle of Corinth and turned plumb mean."

"Did he stay in the rebel army?"

"Yes, sir. The doctors fixed a hook on his right arm so he could grab things. He kilt prisoners at Fort Pillow after they surrendered. Those poor bluecoats knelt down and begged for mercy, but he kilt them in cold blood. They called him Captain Hook."

"Can you describe his hook?"

"It was made out of iron, curved like this and sharp at the end." Rufus bent his finger in the shape of a half circle.

"Doyle, let me see that fragment from Fogarty's skull."

I handed him the sharp metallic sliver. Holmes drew the lamp closer, placed the fragment on a slip of paper. He minutely studied the bit of metal with a magnifying glass. I fidgeted and wondered why a small bit of metal was so interesting or important.

"Please sit in that chair and imagine what you would do if I attempted to drive a knife into your mouth," Holmes said.

"I would clench my teeth and resist, moving my head from side to side."

"Exactly. And, unless it was tightly held as the knife was thrust in, your head would move back. As a result, there would not be enough force to penetrate the vertebra."

Holmes clasped the back of my head with his left hand and drove an imaginary knife into my mouth. "The assailant drove the point of an instrument into the back of poor Fogarty's skull and held it, while, with his left hand, he drove the bayonet from left to right into the vertebra. That instrument was without a doubt, the hook that Rufus described."

"Captain Hook, or should I say Captain Spencer, is most definitely our man," I said.

"Quite right, but we must not jump to conclusions without more evidence. Mr. Freeman, what do you know about the people in these white robes?" Holmes asked.

"They's the ghosts of soldiers who got killed in the war. They ride at night and burn crosses and hang poor Negroes that ain't done nothin' wrong. They's used to be found only down South, but now they's haunting the night right here in Chicago."

"Mr. Freeman, let me assure you there is no such thing as ghosts. These people garbed all in white are flesh and blood, just like you or me. Now, please, if you will, give me a moment to think."

Holmes stretched his legs to the fire and for several minutes was lost in thought.

After what was probably no more than five minutes He sprang out of his chair and paced the floor. "Mr. Freeman, do you know the Captain's room number at the hotel?"

"I can find out."

"Arthur, tomorrow purchase a half-pound of gunpowder and two ounces of sulphur. Mr. Freeman, secure a porter's uniform for yourself. And tonight, both of you, please get a good night's sleep. There's work to be done."

Rufus and I nodded in agreement. "Yes, sir."

"Excellent... Gentlemen, the game is afoot."

18 November, 1878

America is a strange county. It is a nation so full of energy and in such a rush to be a world leader, yet still so backward. For example, Americans have the quaint idea that sulphur is a sovereign remedy for many ills including pains, fevers, and upset stomachs. I found sulphur in a chemist shop among other patent remedies. "Take a pinch of the sulphur in a tablespoon full of molasses. You will be set right in no time," the chemist advised.

He, then, kindly directed me to a store that sold gunpowder and a variety of firearms. I could not ignore the irony of visiting a gun shop in order to cure one's ills. I purchased the gunpowder. While paying the bill, I looked longingly at the Winchester rifles, Colt six-shooters, and a wide variety of pistols, daggers, holsters, and all the equipment necessary to subdue wild animals, Indians, and all the other deadly dangers lurking in the wilds of the American continent.

After my recent narrow escapes, I was determined to purchase a weapon to defend myself. The .45 caliber Colt revolver took my fancy, but I settled on an easily concealed two-shot .32 caliber Remington Derringer.

"If you are concerned about personal protection, may I also recommend this item?" the clerk asked. It was a thin, very sharp stiletto about five inches long that would fit into a sheath strapped to one's leg or forearm. It would be instantly available in case of an attack. I thought back to my assailant on the *Devonia* and could not resist. I walked out of the store with the stiletto in a sheath, firmly strapped just above my right ankle under my wool stocking. With a gun and a knife, I felt like the hero, Hawkeye, in my favorite American adventure book, *The Last of the Mohicans*. For the first time since arriving in Chicago, I felt safe.

The rest of the day, I worked in the laboratory with Carl Lindborg. We dissected the intricate tendons and nerves in the hand of our cadaver. Carl was such a good fellow that, after swearing him to secrecy, I told him of my adventures with Fogarty and Dr. McGillicutty.

"Artie, these are violent times here in America. Everything might be quaint and safe in good old Edinburgh, but here we're in the grips of a terrible financial recession. Why do you think I left our farm in Wisconsin? Ever since I arrived in Chicago, there have been strikes and killings over wages and workers' rights. It's worse down South, where people are boiling over with resentment against the carpetbaggers and President Hayes who they think stole the last election." Carl spoke with the fervor of the downtrodden.

"Still, for the sake of Dr. McGillicutty, shouldn't I investigate further?" I asked.

"As your friend, I beg you to be careful . . . With that said, there is nothing I like more than a grand adventure. If you want to be foolhardy and get to the root of these murders, I am the man to go with you and keep you safe," Lindborg said.

Later, Holmes brooded over Carl's words. "The authorities are unable to solve these murders. The Pinkerton detectives scoff at our methods. A less stubborn man would quit right now, but Angus Duncan is paying handsomely to continue our investigations. I trust we shall get to the bottom of this mystery over the course of this very evening."

"But, how?"

"Here is my plan," Holmes said.

A few hours later, Carl and I, wearing our very best suits and smoking fine cigars, strolled into the lobby of the Tremont Hotel. We looked like two fine young dandies out for drinks, dinner, and a night on the town. Stylish ladies and gentlemen were scattered here and there, chatting on stuffed leather chairs. Others were drifting in and out of the dining room. According to Holmes' plan, we settled into a pair of chairs next to a low table in a corner not far from the grand open staircase.

I placed a folded newspaper beneath the table. Hidden inside was a rolled-up sheet of paper holding a small quantity of gunpowder. I had twisted each end of the paper to contain the powder as well as to work as a sort of fuse. When Rufus, dressed in a porter's uniform, raised his hand, I applied my cigar to the twisted end. When it began to sizzle, Carl and I casually strolled towards the entrance.

Just as Holmes had predicted, exactly ten seconds later there was a loud *whoosh*, flying sparks, flames, and a dense cloud of yellow, sulphurous smoke. People ran to and fro, coughing, gagging, screaming, covering their faces with handkerchiefs, and making for the exits.

Almost immediately, a bell clanged and more guests swarmed down the main staircase. Rufus dashed through the smoke and stamped out the flames, but the sulphur continued to smolder.

The smoke cleared, but the pandemonium continued. I noticed a petite lady hurrying down the staircase. Even though her face was covered, there was no mistaking the elegant Emilie Droussard on the arm of a ramrod-straight gentleman wearing a grey suit and gloves.

Porters and clerks scurried about, attempting to restore order. Carl and I waited for a full ten minutes, as instructed, but Holmes did not appear. After a few more minutes of waiting for him Carl and I went from perplexed to deeply worried.

Next thing we knew, as a few guests were venturing back up the grand staircase, Rufus and a girl in a maid's uniform ran up to us. Rufus could barely get out the words, "They killed him!"

"Who?" I asked.

"Mr. Sherlock Holmes!"

"Great heavens!" We ran upstairs and found him lying, absolutely still, in a pool of blood in the corridor outside the open door to room 203.

There was a long gash on the side of his face. With each faint heartbeat more blood pumped out onto the oriental rug in the hallway. He was barely alive. Carl staunched the bleeding with a folded handkerchief pressed against his scalp. I looked into Carl's calm face. He was a natural physician.

"Artie, we must get him out of here."

Right, let's take him to Mr. Duncan's house. Our safest route is down the servants' stairs and through the kitchen out to the alley. Follow me," I said.

I held pressure on the wound while he and Rufus carried Holmes. As we walked through the kitchen, we kept our heads down and tried to ignore the firemen and police who were restoring order. And then, I felt a hand on my shoulder. A burly, red-faced Chicago policeman blocked our way. "Where are you taking this man? Is he alive?"

Carl spoke up. "We are medical students assisting an injured guest, sir. This man is badly injured. We are taking him to the County Hospital."

"Good, carry on," the policeman said. During the journey to Mr. Duncan's house, Holmes moaned in pain and thrashed about.

Carl and Rufus put him to bed. The deep laceration did not reach down to the skull. The profuse bleeding subsided to a slow trickle after I dressed the gash with carbolic gauze and applied a large pressure bandage. I slumped in utter fatigue and was barely aware when Mr. Duncan enquired about the night's events. He quickly arranged for a nurse who spent the night at the bedside.

Would Holmes live through the night? Had I failed him? If I had dressed the wound poorly and it got infected, I could never live with myself.

I managed to put pen to paper and wrote up the day's events, while wondering again at the enigmatic Sherlock Holmes.

19 November, 1878

In the morning, I went straight to the sick room. Sherlock Holmes was sitting up in bed. His usual sallow complexion was pale and wan. His eyes were sunken but, held that great intelligence. There was a bright flicker of life when his gaze turned to me. "Arthur, thank you for saving my life," he said.

"It was really Carl who had the presence of mind to apply pressure to your wound, "I said.

"Either way, I shall recover but it will take time. Arthur, I am in great pain." He gestured across the room to a cabinet. "Dr. Bell left his instruments with me. Please, there is a bottle of laudanum. Pour a bit for me," he said.

The mahogany case was bound with silver clasps and the interior was lined with green velvet. Each instrument, the bistouries, forceps, saws, probes had their place. Next to a bottle labelled carbolic was another of laudanum, a mixture of alcohol and opium, a powerful pain killer. I poured a teaspoonful for Holmes which he took and begged for another. "Now, before the drug takes effect, I must recount my experiences of last night. When the fire alarm sounded, I dashed up the servants' staircase to the second floor undetected. Rufus's lady friend provided a key tor Captain Spencer's room. Just as Rufus said, there was a grey officer's uniform with the insignia of a major general in the closet. My memory is still clouded, but I think there was a white hooded robe and several articles of women's clothing."

Holmes' head drooped on the pillow for a long minute, and he covered his eyes with both hands. "If only I could remember more specifics," said he.

"Were there any documents?" I asked.

Holmes raised a limp hand to his forehead. "Yes, yes, thank you for asking."

"What did the documents say?"

"I remember . . . A list of names . . . Jefferson Davis . . . Wade Hampton . . . It seems to me that the name Beecher was on the list . . . There were other names, but I just can't remember."

"Did you see Spencer's iron hook appendage?"

"No, but the door to the adjacent room was ajar. I remember now. There was a table with retorts, mortar and pestle, various sized bottles and test tubes, and syringes with needles."

"Chemical apparatus and equipment for medical experiments?" I asked.

"Exactly. But, at that very moment, I was struck from behind and was barely able to stagger into the corridor before collapsing and losing consciousness."

"Did you see your assailants?"

"I sensed that there were two large men."

For a moment, his eyes took on a keen twinkle. "Now, this is vitally important. Did you see anyone come down the stairs?" he asked.

"Well, sir, let's see . . ." I paused. "Carl and I were so nervous about setting off the charge of gunpowder that I didn't notice. "There were dozens of people milling about, making for the exits."

"Think hard."

"Ah, yes. There was a man dressed in a grey suit, walking rather stiffly. I am certain Emilie Droussard was at his side. I may have also seen them together the morning we had breakfast at the hotel."

"Was there anything unusual about his right hand?"

"He wore gloves."

"Was the woman holding his right or left arm?"

"I think she was on his right side, holding his right arm."

"Did that strike you as unusual?"

"No."

"Now, Arthur, a man usually offers his left arm to a lady, so his dominant right hand is free."

I saw the trend of his thought. "Then, if his right hand was useless, he would offer his right arm to the lady."

"Exactly. Captain Spencer or, as he is called, 'Captain Hook,' was wearing an imitation hand, covered with a glove. But, why would he be with Emilie? Hmm . . ."

20 November, 1878

Today, Holmes often lapsed into deep sleep and I noted that the pupils of his eyes were pinpoint, indicating his use of laudanum. Was it for pain, or was he purposefully altering his mind?

In the morning, I attended lectures and assisted in the anatomy laboratory at the Rush Medical College. Upon return to the house, I found Holmes huddled with Mr. Duncan. His bandage was askew, but he seemed much brighter. "Arthur, Mr. Pinkerton has resumed his investigation. I provided him with our information but our suspects have absconded from the hotel, leaving no clues as to their destination. Furthermore, two Pinkerton detectives assigned to Mr. Duncan's Chicago, St. Louis and New Orleans's railway have not reported for work. They are presumed dead, victims of this evil cabal."

I helped Holmes to the great drawing room when Allan Pinkerton arrived for consultation.

"These poor devils were murdered to prevent their work in protecting the railways." Pinkerton spoke with a great air of superiority.

"Sir, it is essential to discover the bodies to see if the thyroid gland was removed," I said.

"Listen to me, lad. I know about these things, and their deaths have nothing to do with your ridiculous theory of organ removal."

"But, we have absolute evidence in one case that the thyroid gland was removed, and the equipment Mr. Holmes found could very well have been used to prepare a glandular extract from the thyroid." My Irish was up. The man was a pompous ass.

Mr. Pinkerton ignored my outburst and spread a map of the United States on the desk. He tapped the route of the railway from Chicago to New Orleans. "Whoever has this railroad can move troops to Chicago and control the western half of the country. It is then only one day to transport a Southern army, augmented by communists and Molly Maguires, to seize Pittsburgh and other major industrial cities. The Federal Army is spread thin out west to control Indians. So, if the rebels choose to attack, there is actually very little we could do to stop the South from taking over the country and restoring slavery."

"Does that explain the presence of Captain Spencer in Chicago?" I asked.

"Young man, that is none of your business."

"Allan, you are mistaken. Mr. Doyle has risked his life to unravel this mystery. It is very much his business." Angus Duncan's reply was somewhat testy. I was happy for his support.

"But, he is a foreigner and only a student," Pinkerton retorted.

"I trust him and you must, too, sir." There was a pregnant pause as both men stared at each other and then looked at Holmes.

Finally, Pinkerton nodded. "Oh, very well. After the Civil War the federal authorities charged Captain Spencer with murder for killing soldiers after they surrendered. He escaped to Mexico and joined Maximillian's army, then went to Venezuela where he made his fortune in gold mines. Sadly, the Hayes administration has pardoned all war criminals. He has returned, is dangerous, and is determined to restore the Confederacy."

"Who is Emilie Droussard?" I asked.

"After her husband was killed at Vicksburg she became a Confederate spy," Pinkerton answered.

There was a pause in the conversation until Sherlock Holmes commented. "Our enemies are quite brilliant. If we are to stop these butchers and survive this investigation, I daresay we must be even more clever."

22 November, 1878

The appearance of Holmes had subtly changed. His face was more drawn, and lines had appeared about his mouth and eyes. His hair was darker and unruly. I scarcely recognized him. "You are much changed. Have you developed another illness? I asked.

"Bravo!" He flung down a copy of *The Chicago Tribune*. "Read this."

Holmes watched me read with a twinkle in his eye. "London scholar and eminent scientist, Mr. Sherlock Holmes, who is visiting our city is reported to be seriously ill and near death."

"Why would they write this?"

"Doyle, are you familiar with *Didelphis Virginiana*?"

"Excuse me?"

"You might be more familiar with its common name — the Virginia opossum. When this creature senses danger, he curls into a ball and feigns death."

I thought for a moment and then smiled. "And you intend to play that same game to lure our opponents out into the open."

"Astute, my lad. Quite astute. Maybe my lessons are finally paying off."

Holmes developed another habit, that of reading newspapers from all different states in America. As he reads one paper after another, he discards them into a stack. I have read in the discarded papers about such things as Nez Perce Indians fleeing through Montana to Canada, Texans fighting over the Mexican border, and Irish miners being hanged in Pennsylvania.

I was not at all surprised when he handed over a copy of *The Memphis Daily Appeal*. "They have struck again, Doyle. Look."

He pointed to an article on the third page which mentioned a young man collapsing on the street and his body immediately being removed. And then he pointed to a story on the back page which announced a series of sermons by the Reverend Henry Ward Beecher and the Scots minister, the Reverend James Balfour, on the subjects of slavery and social Darwinism.

"What do you propose we do about it?" I asked.

"I must go there, but in disguise. I owe it to Angus Duncan, to see this through. He has paid a hefty fee to get us here and has entrusted us with solving this enigma . . . But, my dear Doyle, you are under no obligation to continue with what will be a dangerous mission. Feel free to return homer."

"Sir, I will not run home, and besides, I have always wanted to visit Memphis in Tennessee."

"An epidemic of yellow fever has been raging through that fair city since August. Thousands have already died."

"That does not change my mind."

He chuckled. "I expected you would say that . . . And you must know, if you go, Doyle, your life will be in danger and you will have to pose as a Pinkerton man."

"A Pinkerton?"

"You will be disguised and will need a sturdy companion. You will be well paid, and rewarded if this case has a satisfactory outcome."

"I know the perfect bloke."

"Your mate, Mr. Lindborg, I presume?"

"Why, of course."

"It is agreed then. Allan Pinkerton will prepare two sets of papers for you and Mr. Lindborg. The first will establish you as medical volunteers to assist with the yellow fever epidemic, and the second set will identify you as special security agents for the Illinois Central Railroad."

Carl was eager for the adventure, and, together, we went to the Pinkerton Detective Agency. It was located in an imposing three-story building with a huge sign along the second story which read "THE EYE THAT NEVER SLEEPS."

When we entered the building, a clerk conducted us to the office of the general superintendent where we signed the payroll and obtained our two sets of papers. The pay was six dollars a day, and our task was to "keep an eye on things." Under no circumstances were we to partake of hard liquor or behave in any way that would dishonor the agency.

On our return, Holmes gave us further instructions. "When you arrive in Memphis, stay at the Peabody Hotel and volunteer to aid the sick. At night, spend time in the saloons, pretend to be intoxicated, and brag about being security officers for the railroad."

"For six dollars a day I can do that," said Carl.

"Wait, sir, is that all?" I asked.

"Above all, always stay close. Never let each other out of your sight and follow one another when you are on the streets. The poison curare primarily affects skeletal muscles. If you ever feel a pinprick, it may be a poisonous needle. You must concentrate on nothing else, but breathing with your diaphragm. That is less affected by the poison. This is a deadly game. You may back out if you wish."

"No, I am armed. We will have no fear of those ruffians."

I spoke with great bravado, but with an undercurrent of fear. And then, despite my determination to put Rebecca out of mind, If she were with the Reverend Balfour in Memphis. I might see her again.

23 November, 1878

Rufus came early to help pack. "Mr. Arthur, those folks down South don't take to strangers from the North. Don't you trust nobody and be careful."

"I shall."

"I want to go with you."

"No, Rufus. You stay with Mr. Holmes."

Rufus bobbed his woolly head. "Guess you is right. I'll stick with the doctor, but they's one white man in Memphis you can trust."

"Who?"

"Mr. Josiah Burk on Second Street."

He then took a common pin out of his wallet and a pinch of black soot wrapped in a scrap of paper. "Hold out your wrist." He dipped the pin in the soot and pricked the inside of my wrist, leaving an almost microscopic black dot. "Show him this mark. He helped slaves escape to the North."

An hour later, Carl and I climbed aboard the crowded smoking car of the *St. Louis Flyer*. It was ten o'clock in the morning as we rattled through central Illinois. Carl was jubilant.

"Carl, how can you be so calm?"

Carl puffed on his El Perfecto cigar and smiled. "In just ten days on this job, I am gonna earn sixty dollars. My pa don't see that much money for a year of hard work. It will save our family's farm and pay for Rush Medical School next year."

"That's all well and good, but you won't be able to collect your sixty dollars if you're DEAD!"

"Doyle, you Scottish worry-wart! We'll be fine . . ."

The never-ending prairie, fields of corn, and sluggish rivers rolled past. Carl never stopped talking, puffing his El Perfecto cigar, and pointing out landmarks. He had a natural understanding of the land and botany. He knew the names of the rivers Kankakee and Illinois, and recognized the small towns. Later in the journey, the land was bleak and flat compared to the braes of Scotland. I felt a pang of homesickness and had images of a girl with red hair in the heather.

24 November, 1878

(I am writing this from memory since I did not have my journal for several days)

It took all day to get to East St. Louis where the train cars were loaded on a ferry boat that crossed the Mississippi River. We pulled into the Relay Depot in St. Louis just after four o'clock in the morning, pretty well covered with grit and soot and hungry as bear cubs. In the depot we had fried egg sandwiches and about the worst cup of coffee I ever tasted.

Our old train needed work, so we got on a new one bound for Memphis. Although, the word *new* probably should not be used since the locomotive had an old pokey engine . . . The train had a coal car, a luggage car, and three passenger cars. One was a smoker, but it was filled. We had to get on the second-class carriage where there were only a few empty seats. I remembered Holmes' last admonition, "Boys, don't get separated," but there was nothing to do. I sat next to a grizzled, bearded old farmer, and Carl found a spot a few seats forward.

The talkative farmer took a chaw of tobacco. "We ain't got nothing to worry about on this train, no sir. There's Pinkertons on board, you know, but they's probably dressed like ordinary folks," said he.

I gulped. If he only knew. "Really? Why would you think there are Pinkertons on board today?"

"To protect all that cotton money. Why else?"

"Cotton money?" I asked.

"Why, every year, bankers up North send a safe full of money to Memphis to buy cotton. And when they do, they always hire extra guards."

The farmer offered a bottle of whisky. I overcame my scruples and glugged a healthy swallow. It was rotten homemade stuff, not like smooth malt Scotch whisky.

We were south of St. Louis. The train wound through hills and over streams and rivers on rickety bridges. I was keeping my eyes peeled for Indians when we entered a dense forest that was what I always imagined America would look like. There were occasional patches of corn and shacks, but, no red men.

When the train stopped at a village, The whole town seemed to be nothing more than a general store, a blacksmith shop, and a few run-down log cabins.

"Ain't nothing but poor folks here. The damn Yankees took everything we had. 'Bout time we drove the dang carpetbaggers back up North where they belong," the old farmer said.

"Were folks hereabouts sympathetic with the Confederates?" I asked.

"You're damn right we were. I reckon things get any worse, we're gonna raise us another rebel force."

The train whistle blew. Carl was sound asleep a few rows away.

The train lurched and swayed on the curves at thirty or forty miles an hour until we came to a hill and down a long curve to a valley. The train was not going more than ten miles an hour between a cliff and a small river. All of a sudden, the air brakes screeched and the train crashed to a stop.

The engine and the coal car slipped off the rails and went into a ditch. Folks in our carriage were jostled and shook. I slammed into the seat in front and the farmer fell into the aisle, but no one was badly hurt.

Men on horseback rode down from the hill, whooping and hollering and swearing something awful. They fired at the train. One shot shattered a window in our car. Suddenly, an ear-piercing

BOOM! came from the baggage car up ahead. Pieces of train flew in the air then rained down to earth. The bandits continued shooting guns and whooping.

"Are those wild Indians?" I asked.

"Nah, them be the James boys. They blew the safe. Good for them."

Women screamed and children cried. Everyone tried to hide their valuables. I checked my little pistol and felt for the stiletto. Should I make a brave stand and take out one of the bandits? Pretty soon, two men carrying large revolvers, their faces covered with masks, strutted into the carriage. One fellow was tall, skinny, and sandy-haired, and the other was big-bellied and wore a black, broad-brimmed hat.

The tall, skinny fellow pulled down his scarf to reveal whiskers and a snub nose. "You folks just stay still, put your hands up, and no one'll get hurt."

He held his revolver to the conductor's head and pulled back the hammer.

"Show me them Pinkertons."

"Yes, sir, Mr. James." The conductor pointed first at Carl and then at me. I tried to pull the .32 Derringer from my coat pocket, but the old farmer grabbed my arm. "Put that damn pea shooter away before you get us all killed."

"But —"

"Shush your mouth. That there fellow is Jesse James."

James and his partner came down the aisle, smiling and joking as if they were having the best time in the world. The dark-haired, fat gent carried an open feed sack. He stopped before a rather plain-looking woman and smiled as if she was a real looker. "Please, ma'am, put your money and jewelry in the bag."

Jesse James was polite as he could be to the passengers, but he turned mean and surly when he stopped at my seat. "So, this is one of those damn Pinkerton fellas? I oughta blow off your damn head!"

I hunkered down and tried to look innocent. Carl, blazing with his hot temper, rose to his full height. "The name's Carl Lindborg, and I'll lick you and your whole gang."

Jesse smiled. "You can start by licking my ass," he answered.

James and his gang howled with laughter. Jesse poked his revolver into Carl's ribs. "This here Colt can blow a hole right through your gut. Say one more word and you are dead meat."

I threw aside caution. "Mr. James, please don't shoot! He likes to talk tough, but we aren't Pinkertons. We're both medical students going to Memphis to help with the yellow fever victims."

James jammed his big Colt revolver into my ribs. "Your accent sounds like that blowhard Pinkerton."

"Aye, I'm Irish, but grew up in Scotland and proud of it."

"Pinkerton can't get men no more, so he gets boys to do his dirty work, eh?"

"Lemme kill 'em, boss," the fat gunslinger begged.

"Nah, they might come in handy later." He trained the revolver first on me, then on Carl. He pulled back the hammer and squeezed the trigger. I figured Carl was a goner, but the revolver made a harmless click. Carl went pale as a sheet. Jesse grinned. "Scared, aintchya? If you boys are good, I might let you live a while longer. Some fool might be willing to pay ransom for your sorry tails. Take off them duds and your shoes, so you won't get any ideas about escaping."

"No, we ain't gonna —" Carl protested.

Jesse whacked his mouth with the butt of the heavy revolver, leaving a trickle of blood running down Carl's chin. Carl's eyes went blank, but he did not pass out. We sat down on the floor of the car and pulled off our shoes, then our pants and coats. The fat man kicked me in the ribs. "Shirt, too."

The gang collected more loot from other passengers, then herded us off the train like sheep. I silently thanked Maw for making me wear heavy wool underwear and that she had knitted my stockings out of good Scottish wool. Fortunately, my stiletto, our only weapon, was still strapped to my ankle under the stocking.

The gang stuffed jewelry, greenbacks, and gold pieces into their saddle bags. The big-bellied fellow aimed his pistol at Carl's chest. "C'mon Jessse, lemme kill 'em both right now before we go," he said.

Jesse James looked us over. "Nah. Let's keep 'em as carrots to attract those Pinkerton donkeys. We'll let their stink fill the air. That damn Allan Pinkerton'll come sniffing around. When he does, we'll set a trap and nail that Scottish bastard."

They tied my hands with flat leather thongs and lifted me onto the rump of a horse behind the saddle. When they bound my feet under the horse I was helpless.

They did the same to Carl and we set off on a hard ride. We mucked about through dense woods. Then, one of the gang members yelled to another to go up a stream bed so as not to leave tracks. I tried to imagine I was a character in a great American adventure novel by James Fenimore Cooper. I was not used to praying, but I sure prayed that these desperate men would take pity and turn us loose.

Every so often we stopped so one of the boys could look back for a posse. We were up in the hills where it was colder and snowing. I shivered, and my hands were numb from the tight thongs. It was not until after we came to a ramshackle log cabin that one of the gang finally cut my feet loose. I fell to the hard ground. It hurt, but nothing was broken. We could not walk, so they dragged us into the cabin and shoved us into the corner on the dirt floor. Jesse tied us together with a lariat and hitched one end to a post. We were not going anywhere soon . . .

The musty cabin, lit by one oil lamp, was foul from grease, old sweat, and sour piss. We were tired and thankful to still be alive. I struggled to stay alert and remembered Dr. Bell's admonition to be observant. I hung my head so as not to attract attention, but let my eyes rove around the room, searching for a means of escape. It was a plain log cabin with a low ceiling and two small windows. A table cluttered with whisky bottles and cards was in the middle of the room surrounded by homemade split wood chairs. An iron cook stove and a kitchen counter were near to the door. Straw sleeping pallets were scattered about on the floor, but there was no other furniture. I noticed the gang had hung their coats on pegs by the door, but they kept their guns close by. I did not see any hole where we could slip through and escape.

Carl and I rested our heads upon each other's shoulders, and drowsed off in an exhausted sleep.

25 November, 1878

Come morning, I woke up to the smell of cooking grease and the sound of Carl's snoring. A bedraggled old woman fried corn meal mush, eggs, and pork belly on the stove.

The left sleeve of her dark brown dress was pinned up just below the elbow. The poor woman had no forearm.

Carl awoke and blinked the sleep from his eyes. "Look . . ." he said.

In the opposite corner of the cabin, a man tossed and turned on a straw pallet with his foot poking out from under a pile of quilts. The red, swollen foot was partly plastered with a brown mush. The fellow mumbled about escaping from jail and hiding in the woods, but he did not make sense. He was plumb delirious.

I figured they would give us a scrap of food, but Jesse and his gang ignored us. The gang ate their breakfast on the rickety wood table. There was not a morsel left after they were done eating and scraped their plates on the ground outside the door. We heard the sounds of saddles slapped on the backs of their horses, and then hoofbeats, when they rode away.

Carl and I were alone in the cabin with the wounded man and the old lady. As the day progressed, the old lady bustled about while the wounded man moaned and hollered. I had not had anything to drink for almost a whole day, but had to pee so bad, I almost bust. "It's just a dirt floor, let it go," said Carl. I did and felt a lot better. The smell was no worse than the rest of the room.

Just at dusk the gang returned and flung a small deer on the ground. The old lady, with one hand and the stump of her other arm, skinned and gutted the animal while the men smoked and passed a whisky bottle. Later, our mouths watered while the men ate venison stew. We were powerfully hungry, but they did not even give us scraps.

As everybody ate, the room grew warmer, I sensed an opportunity. I pointed at the injured fellow. "What happened to him?" I asked.

"Got shot in the foot after robbin' a bank last week," said Jesse.

"What's that brown stuff on his foot?" Carl asked.

"A plaster of chewin' tobacco," said the dark-haired fellow with the big belly, who they called Cole Younger.

"He looks pretty bad. Why don't you let us have a look? I wasn't lying. We really are training to be doctors," I said.

"Just listen to the lies. Ma, do they look like the Pinkertons that killed Archie? I should shoot them right now," said Jesse.

I leaned close to Carl. "What's he talking about?" I asked.

"The Pinkertons thought they had Jesse and his gang trapped and blew up his house, but Jesse got away. They killed his little brother, Archie, and his mother lost her arm. Most folks down here sympathize with him and hate the Pinkertons."

Mrs. James lifted the oil lamp close to our faces with her good hand and looked closely into our eyes. "Naw . . . These are just two scared boys. Don't look like no Pinkertons to me."

Our medical training might save us if we convinced these desperados that we could save the life of the injured man. Trouble was we did not have antiseptics or ether or even clean bandages. But, if given the chance, we could make a show of treating the wound and hope they didn't know the difference.

"We got to string them up anyway, on account of they know too much," Cole Younger said.

The injured man was delirious. He let out a piercing cry of pain.

"Hell, Cole, what's the rush? Maybe they can help Ace. Untie their hands and give them a chance to show what they can do," the old lady said.

Her word was law. Jesse untied our hands and held the lamp while we looked at the foot. The bullet had left a big hole that oozed pus just below the ankle. The whole foot was swollen, red, and hot, with red streaks running up the leg. A chaw of tobacco was sticking out of the hole and tobacco juice was smeared over the wound.

My heart sank right down to my socks. It looked hopeless until Carl spoke up in his best country accent. "Thank you, Ma'am. Now, please boil up a kettle of water and give us a bottle of that there whisky. We'll have your boy right as rain in no time flat!"

We cleaned the wound with soap and water and poured whisky into the jagged hole. It still looked bad. The edges of the skin were green and the sole of the foot bulged. I thought even Dr. Bell could not help this man.

"There's pus in there," I said.

"Ma'am, we just need us a sharp knife to drain that there pus," Carl said. I thought of the stiletto still strapped to my leg under my long johns, but did not dare mention it.

The old lady hunted through the shelves and came up with a straight razor. "Here, take this. It's sharp, but don't get no ideas. If you even think of using it for anything other than helping Ace, Jesse will blow your head off."

"Yes, ma'am," Carl said.

Carl plunked the razor in the boiling water and then fished it out with a couple of forks. When the razor cooled, Carl felt the swelling and squinted a long time at the evil mess of torn, infected flesh. Ace had passed out from the fever and hardly moved when Carl made a cut that went across the sole of his foot.

I was pretty nervous until he sliced deeper down to bone and about a pint of green stinking pus welled up out of the wound. We poured in more whisky and tied the foot up in a bandanna that had been boiled.

Jesse's mother nodded. "You boys know doctoring all right. Mebbe we should put you to work and keep you around for a while."

"Hell no. Don't make no difference. They seen our faces. We gotta string 'em up in the morning," Jesse said.

"Why wait? Let's have a necktie party right now," Cole Younger, the meanest man of the bunch, waved his pistol.

"No, damn it. Just tie them up," Jesse said. Cole, the drunkest of the gang, tied our hands, but he fumbled the knots. I could have slipped my hands out of the binding, but waited until the gang finished playing cards and drinking whisky. They finally settled down on the dirt floor for the night at what I judged was about one o'clock in the morning.

26 November, 1878

They were snoring up a storm when Carl gave me a nudge. "Doyle, this might be our only chance."

I worked my hands loose, got out the stiletto and cut the knots on Carl's thongs. He untied my feet and we crawled towards the door. We each took a heavy coat from the pegs and escaped out the door. It had not stopped snowing and it was cold. There was white everywhere. The gang could easy follow our tracks.

"Let's steal a horse," I said.

"They would catch us in no time. We've got to stay in the deep woods. Listen close. These nights are cold, and the snow half-melts during the day, but freezes over with a crust at night. It will be hard for them to follow us on foot or horseback, but I got an even better idea," Carl whispered. He stopped by an old whisky barrel behind the shed.

"What are you doing?" I whispered.

"Going to make a way for us to slip away on top of the crust and move at a faster clip."

Carl ripped away the rusty metal bands that encircled the barrel and removed four curved staves. We listened, but there was no sign the gang heard us. Carl sneaked back into the cabin. In a moment, he returned with a skillet covered with old bacon grease and a coat pocket filled with bread and hunks of venison. "There was still food left on the stove," he said. He smeared bacon grease on the bottom of the staves. "Keep those leather thongs. And now take your skis and let's get going," he said.

"Skis? What are skis?"

"Those staves."

"Huh?"

"I'll explain later. Just grab 'em and follow me."

We tramped off through the snow, but it was bloody cold and hard going. We were leaving tracks, but I was more thankful than ever for Maw's heavy wool stockings and the woolly long johns. The stolen coat helped a lot. At the top of a hill, we stopped at a narrow path that led into the woods.

"Use the thongs to tie your feet to the staves and we will zoom down this hill."

"Carl, I have never been on skis," I said.

"Ain't no time for lessons. Do as I do. Aim your feet downhill and push off," he said.

I felt clumsy but followed Carl down the hill at an alarming speed. We had no more started than I heard shouts and the *BAM! BAM!* of Colt .45 revolvers and the sharp *CRACK!* of a Winchester rifle. They were probably firing at the noise we made. Even though I am writing this a week later, I can still feel the wind as a bullet whistled next to my ear. Fortunately, the gang was still at least half-drunk, and the muzzle blasts must have ruined their night sight.

We slid into a dense stand of brush and trees and were out of their sight, but the gang kept shooting.

I fell down in a snow drift and struggled to get back up. "Crouch low, keep the staves parallel, and bend your knees." Carl said. We started down the hill and I fell to the side, but I righted myself and held my arms out to try to not fall.

I imitated Carl, crouched low, and whizzed down the hill. Despite our being earthbound, it felt as if we were flying. I gained speed, but the gang must have heard us again as they started another barrage of gun fire. I heard one bullet whiz through the brush. I ducked.

Carl reached the bottom of the hill first. He stopped, discarded his staves, and grabbed me as I zoomed by him. "Get rid of your skis and follow me," Carl said. We took off into the dense woods.

Over the course of my short life, I have spent very little time in the country and no time in the deep woods, so I was not feeling especially confident. After a few minutes we did not hear any more shooting.

The sound of howling replaced the sound of bullets. My thoughts turned to wolves and bears and how they might be more dangerous than the gang. But, Carl was comfortable in the deep woods. He forged ahead through the snow, so I stumbled along in his path.

"Carl, do you know where we are going?"

"Don't worry your Scottish head. This is nothing. Once my little brother and I were hunting and got lost in a snowstorm, but we kept warm by moving and survived. By the time we got back to the farm my parents thought we were dead. Keep moving. We will find a stream and follow it until it leads to a river. There are always towns on rivers."

It was dark and terrifying in the forest. And cold. My feet felt like they were solid chunks of ice. Carl kept up a steady conversation — much ado about nothing — which went something like this:

"Arthur, in a fight, who do you think would win; Natty Bumppo — you know, Hawkeye from *The Last of the Mohicans* — or Ivanhoe from Sir Walter Scott's book?"

"Nobody, Carl. They are both fictional characters."

"I know. But, still, if they were in the woods and had to battle to the death, who do you think would win?"

"I refuse to have this inane conversation, Carl. They are not real people."

"All right, then. If Genghis Kahn and Alexander the Great met each other here in the woods and had to fight to the death, who do you think —"

"They lived in completely different eras. It would be physically impossible for them to ever meet."

"I know. But, still, what if . . ."

He kept me awake and going, but I was exhausted. I, grew careless, and tripped over a root. Carl bent down and offered me a ham-sized hand. "Carl, let's rest here for a few minutes," I pleaded.

I pulled the canvas coat tighter. We huddled close together for warmth and rested a few minutes, but the cold was still brutal. Carl's teeth chattered. "We have to go before we freeze to death," he said.

We struggled on together through the black night. Carl talked and talked so we would stay awake and keep our spirits up. Though we eased our hunger by sharing small bites of the food we had stolen from the James Gang, we had no relief from the cold until the early morning sun warmed our cheeks and the snow started to melt.

We stopped going long enough to sit down with our backs to a chestnut tree and chew some chunks of hard bread and venison. Carl got sort of dreamy and talked about his hopes of marrying a pretty nurse and being a country doctor in Wisconsin. That got me to thinking of Rebecca, and my heart warmed.

We got up, stiff and cold, and kept going until we came to a bubbly creek flowing over smooth sand. Our wool socks were already wet and crusted with ice and snow, so we waded into the creek, figuring it would lead to something bigger. The water felt almost warm; at least it was not freezing. We pushed aside brush and stumbled over stones as we walked. My feet felt almost warm for a spell, but soon were, again, like chunks of ice. By that time, my head was sore and my leg muscles burned. I was in a foul mood and wanted to go back to Scotland. This was a lot more adventure on the American frontier than I had bargained for. .

"As long as we continue downstream we will come to a town." Carl was reassuring and I felt better. We rested a while under a big cottonwood tree, soaked up the warm sun, drank cold stream water, and finished off the bread and meat.

"Let's get going. If we can figure which way is east, we will come to the Mississippi river after a while, if we don't reach a town first," Carl said.

It was mid-afternoon when the creek went under a bridge on a dirt road. I collapsed with my back against the base of the bridge. "Carl, I'm sorry, but my feet are frozen and I can't go one step further."

He slumped down next to me. After we had been sitting for a wee bit we heard the sound of a wagon creaking down the road. I thought of the James Gang and felt a stab of fear in my gut, but it was only a lad of not more than sixteen years old driving a hay wagon drawn by a sway-backed mule.

"You fellers look plumb worn out," the boy said.

"Worn out, cold, and hungry. We were robbed in a train holdup," Carl said.

"Where you headed?" The lad asked.

"Memphis."

"That's an awfully long walk."

"We were hoping to get to the river. Can you give us a ride?" Carl asked.

"Naw, the load is already too heavy and I got to get this hay to Cape Girardeau."

I looked the boy square in the eye and pulled the stiletto from under my stocking.

He threw up his hands. "Now fellers, don't cut me."

"I don't mean you no harm. I'll trade this knife for a ride and something to eat," I said.

He admired the sharp killing blade, took the knife, and turned it over in his hand. "Well, ok, fellas. Climb on if you want and I'll take ya. And have some bacon. You can lay back there in the hay and cover up with this here blanket."

Cold bacon never tasted better, and the hay and blanket warmed our bones. The cart clacked and bucked its way over the dirt trail while we huddled together to stay warm. I watched the green woods of Missouri pass by until it got dark. The boy pulled off the road and we spent the night, warm as bugs, under the hay.

27 November, 1878

We arrived in Cape Girardeau at around nine o'clock in the morning. The lad, whose name was Travis, gave us bread and molasses for breakfast. It was still cold, so he let us keep the blanket.

We got off the wagon at the livery stable and limped through town towards the river. A pot-bellied fellow with a shiny badge swaggered towards us. He hooked his thumbs in his belt. "We don't want no good-for-nothing tramps in our town. Beat it or go to jail," he said.

"We aren't tramps. My family owns a 40-acre farm in Wisconsin," Carl replied.

"You damn well look like tramps. Get the hell out of town."

We skedaddled on out of town to the steamboat landing on the great muddy Mississippi River.

I sat on a bench overlooking the river, and, after a few minutes, fell asleep. Carl went off talking to the roustabouts until he met a bloke from Wisconsin who got us a job shoveling coal on a decrepit little cargo steamboat. The captain was glad to have new hands and gave us some old clothes to wear. We were still in our stocking feet, but did not look any worse than the other coal stokers.

We took turns all day shoveling coal into the furnace to keep the steam boiler going. The boat chugged along, stopping every so often to take on bags of grain bound for Memphis. Whenever we could, we snuck out to the deck to get a glimpse of our surroundings and watch the river roll by.

I wanted to write about the journey, but did not have paper or pencil. Instead, I kept the river, the flocks of ducks, and the muddy banks in my memory for a future story. Whenever the fire got low, the first mate cussed and threatened to throw us overboard. I threw big chunks of wood and coal on the fire and ran back on deck so as not to miss anything.

When our shift was over the first mate let us eat leftovers, mostly fried catfish and cornbread. We drank river water after the mud settled and bedded down on grain sacks where we slept like dead men.

28 November, 1878

We did shifts in the morning and afternoon until, in the distance, I made out buildings and tall church steeples up on a bluff. Memphis looked like a fine city, but down by the river there were tumbled-down stores and shacks on muddy streets.

The deckhands lowered the gangplank down onto a cobblestone landing where steamboats were lined up for near a half-mile. The mate gave us burlap bags to wrap around our feet. "I'll pay you two bits apiece if you help us unload," he said.

Carl and I fell in with the black deckhands and passed the hundred-pound sacks of corn to the next man in the line up to the warehouse. I was strong from playing rugger and rounders, but it was bloody hard work.

Big Bart, a six-foot-four black man, was the leader of the workers. "You the first white boys I seen who know how to work," he said.

We all jollied and joked and had a pretty good time. After we collected our two dimes and a nickel I sat next to Bart who offered me an apple.

"You sound British?" he asked, as we ate together.

"I'm of Irish blood, but I'm studying medicine in Scotland."

"So what brings you to these parts?"

"We were robbed by the James Gang. Lost everything and we need help. A friend said we should see Mr. Josiah Burk in Memphis. Ever hear of him?"

"No." Bart turned cold and distant. "I don't know no Mr. Burk."

"Well, do you at least know where Second Street is?"

"Don't know that neither."

Bart got up to leave, but I grabbed his shoulder. I showed him the black spot on my wrist. He paused and squinted. "Who made that mark on you?"

"My friend, Rufus Bubba Freeman."

"He must have been a slave at one time."

"Yes. That's right. He used to be known as Rufus Bedford Forrest."

His face crinkled with a big smile. "In that case, you keep on this here road until you are up on the bluff and come to Second Street. Turn right and go down a ways. Mr. Burk lives in the white house."

It was near dark when we found the white cottage surrounded by old trees.

"We better go around to the back door, especially considering we're still wearing these dirty old rags from the steamer," Carl said.

I hung back and let Carl do the talking when a little old lady opened the door just a little. "You men looking for food?" she asked.

"No, Ma'am, I'm a Wisconsin farm boy, and now, we're medical students coming to help with the epidemic. We were robbed and come to see Mr. Josiah Burk," Carl said.

The lady opened the door another few inches and squinted at us through little half-rim spectacles. She could not have stood more than five feet tall. She wore a bonnet and a long calico dress buttoned up to her neck.

"Land-sakes, you boys look a fright."

I guess we did look pretty bad. My shirt and long-johns were soot-covered and torn. The fact that we did not have shoes made us look worse than the usual tramp. Carl was in just as bad a shape and neither one of us had washed or combed our hair in a week. "Come in, come in, and I'll call my husband," she said in a kindly soft voice.

She took us into her warm, cheery kitchen lit by two oil lamps and heated with a big iron cook stove. We both drooled at the sight of a big piece of ham, a loaf of bread, and a bowl of apples on the table.

"Josiah, two boys are here to see you."

Mr. Burk was a stout man with hair gone to grey and dressed in a black frock coat, shiny black trousers, and a white shirt. He looked solemn enough to be a minister, but, after he said thee and thou a few times, we learned that he and his wife were Quakers. I held out my wrist towards the lamp so that they could see the tiny black spot.

"Remarkable. I have never seen that mark on a white man."

"A black man said we could trust you," I said.

He stroked his beard. "Mrs. Burk and I helped many a slave to freedom before the war."

The Burks gave us supper, and Mrs. Burk drew a hot bath. After Carl scrubbed down with rough, homemade soap I jumped in while the water was still hot. It felt so good to be clean and warm. Our bedroom was a lean-to out back with only one sofa. Carl took the floor. "Sleeping on a nice warm hardwood floor is nothing," he said. "Back on the farm, we had so little room in the house, I'd often sleep on the dirt floor of our chicken coop."

In minutes, Carl snored. I could not sleep, so I wandered to the kitchen. Mrs. Burk was reading a religious tract. I slumped down on a wooden kitchen chair across from her.

She had white hair and watery, sad grey eyes that reminded me of my dear, poor mother.

Mrs. Burk poured boiling water from a copper kettle onto dry tea leaves in a plain white cup. "Drink this," she said.

It was a dark, strangely soothing brew. In a moment, I emptied the cup and felt drowsy. She took the cup, swirled the remaining leaves, and looked intently at the bottom and sides of the cup.

Her old grey eyes took on a new luminosity. I sensed a change in the room and the intensity of her gaze. "You are troubled by a dark, inky past. For a young man, you've experienced great sadness and much death. It's your Irish blood and the Romani blot."

Her voice was a mere whisper, but every word went into my very soul.

I shivered at the memories of the harsh beatings and my rigid education at the hands of the Jesuits when I was a boy. I had forsaken religion for science, a move that caused my Maw great sorrow.

Mrs. Burk looked back down into my teacup. "I see an older woman — dying. Your grandmother, perhaps. You're just a young boy, crying at her bedside."

The shock of my grandmother's death came back with the full force I had felt while still a young boy. Her passing started our family on the path to poverty and ruin, and it was the reason I was sent away to live with relatives and the Jesuits.

"Now I see another woman, a wisp of a girl, but beautiful. She tugs at your heart, but she is not of your faith and would bring great sadness to your mother. You must not marry her."

I came alert with a start. My mind whirled. Did this old woman have the gift of second sight? Could she see the past and divine the future? My scientific background and Jesuit teaching told me no. But, then, was she speaking of my dear Rebecca? I was overcome with shame and guilt that took my breath away. I had abandoned the faith of my parents, and I had eagerly run away on this trip, leaving them in their poverty. I should have stayed in Edinburgh to help out.

I felt awful. How could I be such a bad son? I stumbled away and sank into bed.

29 November, 1878

I awoke on the sofa to the smell of bacon and sausages that reminded me of home. It took a minute to realize I was in the middle of perilous America. Mrs. Burk had generously mended our clothes, so we looked halfway decent for the first time in days. The Burks also had a storeroom with old clothes and shoes for runaway slaves that they now shared with poor travelers like us. I found a pair of boots that almost fit. A little lamp black made them look respectable.

"So, you boys want to use your medical learning to help with the yellow fever?" Mr. Burk inquired while we were at breakfast.

"Yes, sir," we answered.

"The epidemic is almost over, but there still are sick folks at St. Mary's who need help."

"Was there a lot of fighting around here during the war?" I asked.

"Oh yes. The Union took Memphis early in the war, then the Rebels raided the fort several times," Mr. Burk said.

"Ever hear of a Confederate officer named Captain Hook?"

"He was bad. A very bad man. Funny you mention him. I just overheard some folks saying that he is rallying his old troops to make mischief again."

"Sir, I can do chores or give you a nickel for a notebook or a pad of paper and a pencil."

Mr. Burk rummaged through an old roll top desk and produced a pad of cheap foolscap and a pencil stub. "It's worth a nickel," he said.

I thanked him, took the paper, and offered to do chores, but he sent us on our way with handshakes and smiles.

The imposing St. Mary's was a big stone structure with a high steeple that had been made into a hospital. The yellow fever epidemic might have been nearly over, but there were still at least fifty poor, sick souls lying on cots in front of the altar. A nun in starchy white met us at the door. She looked us over with a critical eye.

"Do you boys have medical experience?" she asked.

"Yes, Ma'am. We are medical students and want to help."

She pointed to a heap of wrapped bodies. "First thing, carry out the ones that died last night."

The corpses were already wrapped in sheets and light as a feather. When we finished stacking the bodies on the cart like so much cordwood, another sister gave us buckets of water and towels to clean new patients.

All day, we cleaned black vomit, changed beds, and held patient's heads while they took broth. It was more like nursing than medical work, but it felt good to help these unfortunate souls. No matter how awful my problems seemed to be, these folks had it much worse.

The new patients were out of their heads with fever, their teeth chattered from chills, and they bled from their mouths, eyes, and noses. The skin of some patients had turned yellow, and even I could see that many were doomed to die from kidney or liver failure.

It was late afternoon when Carl and I took a break and rested on a cot. A nice-looking lady holding a pot of coffee sat down next to us. "You boys must be plum tuckered out. Have some coffee," she said.

"Thank you, ma'am," said Carl.

She poured each of us a cup. "This is the first time I have seen you boys."

"We're medical students from Chicago," I said.

"They say the epidemic is about over. Good thing, since my gals are getting tired of seeing these poor folks die every day. The sisters pray for their souls, but there ain't much else we can do," she said.

"It's awfully hard, but important, work," I added.

"Where are you boys staying?"

"We don't have lodgings yet," I said.

"If you behave and leave my girls alone, I can give you a meal and make room for you at my place. Go to Angie's Hotel on First Street right on your way to the docks. Go in by the back door and say Angie sent you."

"That's very kind," I said.

"There was a nurse with a funny accent like yours who was here yesterday."

"Did she happen to have flaming red curly hair and sparkling green eyes?" I asked.

"Why, yes, she did."

"Was her name Rebecca?"

"I think so."

My heart skipped a beat. "Do you happen to know where she might be staying?"

"She didn't say."

I had vowed to give up on Rebecca, especially after Mrs. Burk's strange message that had gone straight to my heart. Yet I could not get her out of my mind as I blindly followed Carl through darkened streets. It was raining and the wind was whistling off the river when we finally came to First Street.

The area was mostly lit by red lanterns in front of dismal shacks and saloons. Angie's Hotel was a higher-class place, though not by much. The kitchen was clean, but the cook, an old black lady with an enormous apron across her fat belly, was not very friendly.

"Why ain't you usin' the front door, like every other man?" she asked

"Angie sent us here."

"I 'spose you wants eats?"

"Aye, a bit of food would be much appreciated," said I.

"I kin give you beef stew and fixin's for fifteen cents."

We shelled out thirty cents in dimes and nickels and tucked into beef stew, homemade biscuits, and gravy served out of tin plates at the kitchen table. The cook sat with us. "These are the best vittles I've had in a long time," Carl said.

She smiled for the first time. "You kin call me Ma, like all the girls. You boys is more polite than most men who come here. Would you like a helpin' of apple pie?" she asked.

"Yes ma'am," I said.

She served up two slabs of pie filled with sliced apples, cinnamon, and sugar. "Oh, I've never, even at home, had such good pie," said Carl.

"Yes, it is quite lovely," I added.

"Nobody ever called my pie lovely 'afore," she said.

"How's business?" Carl asked.

She sighed. "Ain't been much of anything you can call business since the epidemic, 'cept last night when a crowd of old Confederates come nosin' around. I din't like them fellers at all."

We were scraping the bottoms of our plates and licking our spoons when a little, blonde, skinny girl flounced into the kitchen wearing a wide-open, tiny housecoat without a stitch of underclothes except for black stockings and loose slippers. She was no more than sixteen years old if she was a day. The girl acted like we were not even there. "Ma, kin you let me have a pitcher of warm water for washin'?" she asked.

The cook filled her pitcher from a bucket on the stove. Then, the little, blonde girl acted like she had just noticed us. "Oh my. Well, hello there, gentlemen. Are you boys lookin' for fun?"

Carl and I smiled shyly. "Sorry, ma'am, but you see we're Pinkerton agents on official railway business," said I.

"I don't care if you're the crown prince of Wales. You oughta be in the front room with the girls."

Carl cleared his throat, but could not speak. She gave Carl a lascivious smile, twitched her hips, and sat down on his lap. "Hello there, Curly. You big, beautiful, sweet boy. Do you mind if I sit down for a minute?" She kicked a leg back and forth and played with a lock of Carl's hair.

"Um, eh . . . Ah . . ." Carl stammered.

"Curly, I ain't got nothin' to do tonight and I'm sure lonely. Why don't you follow me to my room? I can sure show you a good time . . ."

Carl's face turned beet-red and his jaw started to work, but all that came out of his mouth was hemming and hawing. "Hmm . . . Emm . . . Ummm . . . Ah, sorry, ma'am. You seem nice and all, but we best be on our way." Carl jerked up to his feet and the little girl practically fell to the floor.

"Now, Curly, you ain't very sociable."

"You can stay as long as you want and socialize, but I got things to do," Carl said to me.

Carl burst out the front door. I was sort of reluctant to leave, but followed him into a pouring rain. Carl's face was still flushed with a rosy hue and I could not help but laugh at him.

"What's so funny?"

"I've seen you stand up to Jesse James, but one little girl made you squirm like a wee lad with ants in his knickers," I teased.

"Well, um, eh, that there place is one of those houses of ill repute. We might have gotten a disease if we stayed there too much longer," said Carl.

"Carl, you can't catch venereal diseases from food and furniture."

"Still, it was, um . . . Well . . . I've never done . . . You know . . . and I'm gonna save myself for my wedding night, and I don't wanna talk about this no more!"

Misty halos formed around the gaslights and the eerie light made for a dreadfully unnerving feeling. I looked back over my shoulder at every little noise and jumped at the clatter of hooves and jingling spurs. A troop of fifteen or twenty men on horseback cantered down the street, two abreast. Every man wore a long red shirt, carried a rifle, and had a set, dark expression.

"Keep your head down and walk straight ahead," Carl said.

"Who are those men?"

"Red Shirts. One of the White Militias that go night-riding to scare the blacks."

I grabbed Carl and pulled him into an alley. "Carl, people are talking about Confederates. I thought the war was over years ago."

"The war over slavery didn't really end. The Southerners won't give the black people equal rights. They don't let them vote and, in the end, they want to restore slavery. They say the Republicans stole the last election and Northerners are sick of the whole thing and don't really care what happens."

"So, in a way, the war is still going on."

"You might say that . . . Now, we have to secure our lodgings and get out of this rain."

"Sherlock Holmes said we should go to the Peabody Hotel."

"We've only got ten cents apiece."

"Never mind. It won't hurt to try."

The Peabody was about the swankiest place in Memphis, but we walked right up to the desk like we always stayed in the finest hotels all our lives. "Hello, dear sir. Might there be any messages for Mr. Arthur Conan Doyle?" I asked.

"Why yes," The clerk, without batting an eye, took an envelope and a key with a tag numbered 215 from a cubby hole. The envelope was stuffed with greenbacks, enough for a week's pay for both of us, and a scrap of paper with two words: "Keep quiet."

The door to room 215 was unlocked and did not make a sound when I pushed it open. To our great astonishment, Holmes, smoking his Meerschaum pipe, sat with a binaural stethoscope pressed against the wall. And there was good old Rufus, squatting on his haunches, shining shoes. He had stayed with Holmes just as he promised.

Holmes put his finger to his lips, motioning for us to be quiet, and offered the stethoscope to me. I adjusted the ear pieces and pressed the bell against the wall to hear snatches of conversation and the tinkling of glasses. *"Why not just shoot him . . . It must appear to be a natural death . . . It is perfected . . . That bastard in Chicago knows . . . The depot in . . ."*

I could not make out all the words, but Holmes had a page full of notes. Carl gasped when he saw the names: Wade Hampton, Jubal Early, Martin Cary. We moved away from the wall and spoke in whispers.

"Those are names of Lee's Confederate generals who never surrendered," Carl said.

"They are plotting assassinations as we speak," Holmes said.

There were more notes, something about a Reverend, that I could not make out. "It sounds as if they are planning more assassinations with the curare poison," I said.

Then an awful thought crossed my mind. If "that bastard in Chicago" were Holmes, his life was in great danger.

Or maybe, they were referring to me . . .

Holmes had thoughtfully brought my precious diary, so I am setting down everything I remember since leaving Chicago. I wrote about our narrow escape the James Gang who are not so different from the highland robbers so prominent in our Scottish lore.

Aye, we are in danger, but thoughts of Rebecca, and the possibility of seeing her again, are a tonic.

2 December, 1878

Early this morning, Carl and I went to the cathedral, and I asked about the red-haired Scottish beauty. "Try President's Island. There are more patients quarantined there," a nursing sister finally told me.

Carl and I spent some of our salary on new clothes, cigars, and beer and sandwiches in a saloon, where we listened to the gossip. Recalling our original plan, we let it be known that we were Pinkertons working for the railroad. Everyone shied away as soon as they heard our accents, and one fellow called us *"damn carpetbaggers."* After we left the saloon Carl went back to the cathedral, but I hurried down to the landing to catch a ferry to President's Island.

Once on the island I walked into what seemed to be an old warehouse, which is now a makeshift hospital filled with the worst cases. I looked down a long corridor filled with beds and she was there! Her red hair stood out like a bright star in a dark evening sky.

"Miss Yates?"

She looked up from wiping vomit off a small lad and tossed a limp lock of hair from her eyes. Her voice was dull and tired. "Oh, Arthur, is it really you?"

"Yes, it is me. I found you."

"Oh, Arthur." She fell into my arms and sobbed. "They're all dead. Jimmy is the only one alive."

I held her and tried to soothe her anxiety. It took several moments for me to understand. The Reverend and Mrs. Balfour had died of yellow fever. Jimmy, their son, was here and near death. The poor boy was feverish, delirious. I could barely feel his pulse.

"Rebecca, please, come with me. You are so tired and in danger of contracting this terrible disease."

"No, I must stay with Jimmy to the end."

I begged her to come with me. In Scotland, Dr. Bell would surely look after her and Jimmy, but she insisted on staying with the sick child.

I was torn between staying with Rebecca and going back to Carl and Holmes.

"Do you have a place to stay?" I asked.

"Yes, with the Reverend Beecher who is also not well. I am needed here."

"My friend Holmes is not a doctor, but he almost qualified, I shall bring him to see Jimmy," I said.

I hugged her and left to catch the ferry back to Memphis. Was it fate? Had this terrible disease led to our reunion?

It was dusk when the boat touched the dock in Memphis. As we moored a steam launch backed out into the river. In the fading light, I could make out a tattered sign on the launch which read—THE LOCKE-MEMPHIS LINE. I remembered the bloody words, *cinnte faoi ghlas*. Sure lock. Could that refer to Locke?

The launch steamed downriver, nosing against waves with its stack belching smoke, I sprinted down the dock to see the sign better but the launch was too far away to learn more. A grey-bearded black man was fishing with a long cane pole at the edge of the dock. "Excuse me, sir, may I ask about that steam launch?

The old man looked away. "I don't know nothing bout' that boat," said he.

Then, he pulled in his line, picked up a can of worms and made as if he were in a hurry to get away.

I held out a silver half dollar. "Will this help your memory?"

He snatched to coin and carefully examined the eagle on one side and the lady on the other. "It looks genuwine," he said.

"Now, tell me about "The Locke-Memphis Line," I said.

He scratched his chin, then looked down the river. "Dat is an evile place. Old Massa Locke had a whole island planted in cotton and near about 200 slaves. He done named the plantation after his wife, Shirley, but folks around here called it the 'Sure-Locke' place. Massa Locke his three boys got kilt in the war. His wife done went crazy and kept on fightin' the Yankees. Nobody seen her in five-six years but they is grey coats, rebels stayin' on the place and they's a whole lot of shrieken' and howlin' men with guns, that keeps people off."

"Thank you," I said.

"Don't tell nobody I told you," he said. The old fellow dashed away leaving his pole and worms on the dock.

It had to be the place that poor Fogarty warned about with his bloody, dying hand? I dashed to the cathedral. Carl. He was spooning broth into the mouth of an old man. After he had finished we hurried back to the hotel, anxious to give Holmes the news, but he was asleep with an open bottle of laudanum at his side.

3 December, 1878

At six o'clock this morning, Holmes was reading his newspapers and drinking coffee, as alert as ever. I told him about the Sure-Locke plantation and then about the Balfours.

"Sir, you will remember the Belfours and the girl, Rebecca Yates from the ship," I said.

"Indeed I do," he said.

The Balfours are dead from the fever, and Jimmy is very ill. Rebecca is looking after the boy on President's Island. Can you help the boy?" I asked.

"Oh, so sad, so sad. The Balfour clan is one of the most important in Scotland. Therapeutics is not my strong suit, but I may be able to help," he said. "We must save Jimmy's life."

"A life is at stake. We leave at once."

Holmes hailed a cab. "Hurry, man, to the ferry landing." The ferry was not running. "Hello!" he shouted at men on a fishing boat. "A ten-dollar gold piece for a ride to President's Island."

It took but a quarter hour for the man to row us to the makeshift hospital. We hurried in and dashed past wretches lying in putrid vomit.

"Damn, this is intolerable. We would never stand for this neglect of the sick in England."

Then, like a beacon of light, we came to Rebecca, still at Jimmy's bedside. Her lovely face was streaked with tears and she was worn from overwork. Carl, my big unfettered friend, appeared to be struck dumb when he saw her.

Without a word, Holmes threw off his coat and knelt by Jimmy. The lad was delirious with fever and crying weakly for his mother. His lips were parched and cracked, and his eyes were sunk into his head. It was a dreadful sight. The lad was near to death.

"When did he last drink?" Holmes asked.

"He hasn't had a drop of liquid since yesterday morning. I have tried, but he will not swallow," Rebecca responded.

"We must get him out of here. This is no place for a Scots lad of the great Balfour clan to die. Doyle, wrap the lad in my coat."

I bundled Jimmy and carried him in my arms to the waiting boat. "Doyle, where can we find a quiet place with clean linens, drink, and food?" Holmes asked.

I thought for a second. "There is the cathedral, but it's just as crowded as the quarantine hospital. Everyone in the city is frightened of the disease."

"There must be someplace we can go."

"Let me think. Carl and I met a woman, Angie, a kindly soul, runs a sort of a hotel which is not far away."

"It would not be proper," Carl said.

"Never mind, Angie's is the only place," said I.

During the ride across the river, I thought again of the enigmatic Holmes. He is not a fully trained physician and had rarely shown a streak of human kindness, but he was behaving like an empathetic human being for the first time since we had met. Angie's girls helped us take the sick lad to Angie's room on the second floor.

Angie's room was opulent, with a brightly lit gold chandelier, a frilly four-poster bed, paintings of cherubs on the wall, and a large plaster saint in a lighted niche. Holmes rolled up his sleeves and went to work. "Doyle, soak sheets in cold water and bring a pitcher of lemonade with sugar and salt."

The young girls of the house scurried about fetching sheets and pitchers of ice water. Rebecca soaked the linens in icy water. Carl and I wrapped Jimmy in the sheets. "Hurry! Where is the lemonade? And bring chicken bouillon," said Holmes.

A particularly fetching lass, wearing only a shift, ran into the kitchen and helped Ma, the old black cook, make enough lemonade for half the city. Then Ma took up a kitchen cleaver, went into the backyard, and killed a chicken to make the broth.

We forced lemonade, fortified with whisky, between Jimmy's lips. Most of the drink spilled down his chin, but, eventually, he took the liquid. His teeth chattered with the cold, and his skin took on a bluish tinge, though his temperature receded.

"Ah, we must not go too far. Now, we shall apply warmth," said Holmes.

The girls filled brass bed warmers with hot ashes from the fireplace. We removed the icy sheets, and, with the warmers and blankets, we warmed the boy.

We continued the vigil through the day and into the night. Rebecca slept, slumped in a chair, while we took turns at the bedside spooning lemonade and broth into the boy.

4 December, 1878

Carl was on duty during the dark, wee hours of the morning when human vitality is at its lowest. Jimmy gave one last small sigh and stopped breathing.

Carl put his hand on the boy's chest. "No! The poor fella . . . He stopped breathing!" he shouted.

Holmes, sleeping in a rocking chair, came awake, leaped to Jimmy's side, placed his mouth over the lad's, and forced his own breath into the child's lungs.

After a few moments — moments that seemed like an eternity — Jimmy took a breath, then another. We continued the vigil, which seemed more and more like a death watch. But, in the morning, when sun came streaming through the window, he was no worse.

I had my hand on his feeble pulse. Carl and Holmes closed their eyes and had forty winks. Ma tip-toed into the room with a pitcher of strong root tea. "This is an Indian remedy. Us slaves used it for the fever."

Rebecca and I took turns forcing spoonfuls of the murky brown liquid down Jimmy's throat. By mid-morning, his eyes fluttered and his pulse was stronger. He swallowed more tea and lemonade then drifted into a quiet sleep. By mid-afternoon, Jimmy was able to take an entire cupful of broth and his cheeks had gained a hint of a pink glow.

They said it was a miracle that a child so young had survived a bout of yellow fever. The young ladies of the house were in and out of the sick room, sometimes bringing little treats. But, mostly, they fluttered about Carl, playing with his curly hair and making him blush.

I thought it was the Indian tea. Holmes did not scoff at my thought. "There is more to native remedies than we know. I will perform a chemical analysis when we reach home," he said.

When we left, Angie and her girls made a fuss over the lad. The little blonde girl curled his hair and planted a big kiss on Carl who seemed to have lost his fear of "painted ladies."

Mr. Payne, the Reverend Beecher's host, sent a regal carriage for Rebecca and Jimmy. I wrapped Jimmy in blankets and carried him into the carriage. Rebecca insisted that I accompany them to the Payne's grand mansion.

Half an hour later, we drove through the stately gates and into a grove of old Rowan Oak trees. It seemed as if we rode for another mile until we finally reached the three-story brick mansion. The proud façade featured porticos, tall windows, and a wide veranda. A servant opened the door and welcomed Rebecca.

I carried Jimmy to a third floor room once occupied by the Balfour family. The lad cried for his parents and was weak as a newborn kitten, but his body was mending well.

"The Reverend Beecher will be stopping by in a moment. I'd like you to meet him," said Rebecca.

I had heard and read a good deal about this Reverend Beecher. His sister was the author of *Uncle Tom's Cabin,* and his adultery trial in 1874 was the most famous of the century. In his prime, the Reverend was a tall, handsome fellow with a high forehead and flowing black locks that hung down below his ears.

During his long sermons, Beecher howled high-flown moral platitudes, used slang and humor, banged his fists, and stamped his feet. Even though he was more than fifty years old, he was rumored to still have dashing looks and the romantic air about him of a much younger man. Like many of the women who heard his sermons, I wondered if Rebecca had amorous thoughts about the old lecher.

When the Reverend Henry Ward Beecher greeted us, I was struck by his pallor and how different he looked from what I had imagined. His skin was dry and he lacked vitality. He was sickly, moved with difficulty, and his breathing was labored. He held out a quivering hand when Rebecca introduced me as Dr. Bell's assistant.

"Ah, Mr. Doyle, I am pleased to meet you. Mrs. Balfour regaled us with her praises of you and Dr. Bell. I wonder — is it a coincidence, or God's divine will, that you, the assistant to the great doctor are here in this very city?"

"Dr. Bell has returned to Edinburgh, but Mr. Sherlock Holmes is a brilliant scientist," I said.

"Oh, how disappointing. I am not as young as I used to be and I must gather my strength. I have to complete my great work."

"Mr. Holmes may be of assistance to you."

"Is it true that he just saved the life of young Master Balfour?"

"That is correct," I said.

"Perhaps he would grant me a clandestine consultation. My physician has great faith in glandular extracts, but I want another opinion."

"Who, may I ask, is your physician?"

"Dr. Edward Droussard."

I was taken aback. "Sir, do you mean Emilie Droussard?"

"Not Emilie. Edward. He has a most brilliant scientific mind and he is most up to date in his practice." Beecher grabbed my shoulder. "Droussard is providing me with the very latest treatments to restore my vigor and endow me with eternal youth, but I want to seek counsel from another doctor."

"I will relay your desire for a consultation to Mr. Holmes," said I.

"Excellent . . . Ah, to fly about as if I was a young boy again," the Reverend Beecher said, with a smile.

I offered my farewell to Miss Yates, but she was preoccupied with Jimmy and did not even wish me well.

I was devastated by the cruel, cold distance that she had imposed between us, but I pretended to not be hurt, held my head high, and made my way back to the carriage, never once looking back.

5 December, 1878

At breakfast, in the luxurious Peabody dining room, I attempted to inform Holmes of Dr. Beecher's desire for a consultation. He waved me off. "Have you learned anything of importance?" I told him about the steam launch and the Locke plantation him. He took in my story with a raised eyebrow. Carl then related a conversation, by former confederate officers, overheard by Angie. There was talk of overthrowing the government but they lacked a charismatic leader to convince the Northern states to repeal the Thirteenth Amendment that freed the slaves. They hope that this leader, whoever he is, will become the next President of the United States.

"Carl, there are too many good, God-fearing people in this country to allow such a thing to occur," I said

"Sorry Arthur, but that's not true." Carl shook his head. "Most Northerners are still sick of war and not interested in the plight of former slaves. Many of our leaders are conciliatory towards the Southern whites."

Holmes blew a cloud of fragrant smoke into the air. "Dr. Beecher's desire for a consultation may fit into this puzzle. He has renounced his former abolitionist views and thinks the blacks would be better off as slaves under benevolent owners at least until the twentieth century. He just might be the charismatic leader the confederates are seeking," Holmes said.

"Speaking of the Reverend Beecher, I met him when I went I returned Miss Yates and Jimmy to their lodgings."

Holmes drained his cup of strong coffee, put down his pipe and sprang from his chair. "Aha, yes, poor Fogarty indeed provided the most important clue. The mystery will be solved at the Locke plantation. Doyle, arrange for a boat to convey us down river to reconnoiter this evil place. You, Rufus, find out more about the

Locke plantation," Holmes said. We set about on our assigned tasks and arranged to report to Holmes the next day.

6 December, 1878

After lunch Rufus gave his report. "I had to pay a dollar 'afore anyone talked. Some folks say the place is cursed. Others say it be a house with haunts. Even white folks won't go there."

"Now, Rufus, are these old wives' tales?" Holmes asked

"It's the truth. It was a rich cotton plantation on a piece of low land dat jutted into the river, but da river come up and cut a channel dat made the tip of the land into an island It is cut off and folks claim it is growed up with weeds and bramble thickets and dey's rattlesnakes and wild beasts that walk on two feet and screech somethin' fierce. Dey's an old, scarlet-colored plantation house on a hill with a buncha other little old cabins next to it. Black folks say ghosts of dead Confederate soldiers live dere and when dey's a full moon, da walls of dat place run red with blood, and lights flicker, and Lucifer's smoke pours outta all the winders of dat ole place."

"Doyle, have you found a boat? And where is this place."

"Yes, I can get a boat and it is about fifteen miles downriver," I answered.

"Splendid, we shall reconnoiter this afternoon, but first, I shall attend to the Reverend Beecher."

I hailed a cab and we set off to the mansion. Holmes lit his pipe, and exhaled a fragrant cloud of smoke. "Beecher may lead us to the heart of this mystery and to the sinister mind that lurks behind all of these deaths."

"A valet ushered us to a sitting room where Reverend Beecher reclined on a leather covered armchair.

He appeared weak, but he talked eagerly of his upcoming operation as he walked Holmes to the library. "Have you ever read Ovid's Metamorphoses?"

"No, I don't care for literature. Why do you ask?"

"It is the myth of an eternal child who never grows old. This myth has always meant a great deal to me because as a young boy in

Litchfield, Connecticut, I had a dear, dear friend, Peter, who died at the tender age of eight. He was such a sweet, gentle soul. He was musical and loved to play the pan pipes. When a child dies so young, in the minds of those who loved him he never grows old. It is as if sweet Peter lives on in a never, never land where he is a *puer aeternus* — an eternal youth."

"Reverend Beecher, I'm sorry to say this, but, as a man of science, I find it hard to believe that this operation will give you eternal youth."

"It is my heart's desire. And, mind you, it is not a selfish one. I only dream of it for the sake of salvaging this great country from ruin."

The Reverend Beecher talked about his great work of recanting his original abolitionist views. "I shall convince the North to remedy its mistakes and save the country," he said.

We listened to Beecher talk on an on for what seemed like an hour until Holmes interrupted. "Sir, we must be on our way. May we now return to the topic of your operation?"

"Yes, of course. I am sorry, but politics have become my new religion, so to speak. My doctors have assured me that my ill health is due to a lack of glandular secretions. The injections I've been receiving are not helpful, so the next necessary step is a surgical implantation of tissue directly into my body."

"I am very curious. What is the origin of the glandular extracts?" Holmes asked.

"I presume they are of animal origin."

"The Swiss have had limited success with glandular implants, but only in very specific conditions of proven deficit," Holmes said.

"According to Dr. Droussard, the surgical incision is the only danger. He is willing to do the operation and use the new antiseptic technique. I trust there will be little risk and it would be my pleasure to have Mr. Doyle give the anaesthetic."

Holmes interest quickened at the name Droussard. "I insist on having my entire team, and I must inspect the local hospital facilities."

"It must be done in absolute secrecy. My doctors conduct experiments in a perfectly modern laboratory with suitable facilities for surgery," said the Reverend.

We left the stately mansion without a single glimpse of Rebecca. It was a pleasant Tennessee day. The air was cool and crisp as we walked to the docks. Our vessel was eighteen feet long with four oars, a mast, sail, and tiller.

We set off downriver in high spirits. Carl and I each took a pair of oars. Rufus was at the stern with the tiller. Sherlock Holmes lounged on the bow seat and scanned the shores with a powerful telescope. A contrary southerly breeze precluded use of the sail, but with the strong current we made rapid progress.

After leaving Memphis the shoreline became low with innumerable small creeks and inlets. Holmes pointed out hawks, shorebirds, turtles sunning on logs, otters, and even a black bear on the shore. He knew little and cared less for literature or philosophy, but he was a wizard at all the natural sciences. It was a little after three o'clock in the afternoon when we rounded a bend and saw before us a small heavily wooded island and, much to our surprise, a two-story house — painted a bright scarlet-red.

We shipped our oars and drifted another quarter of a mile while Holmes minutely surveyed the island. He passed the handsome brass instrument to me, and, after adjusting the lens, I examined the island, commencing with the scarlet house and the surrounding scarlet cabins.

The main building appeared to be an old-style Southern plantation house, and the cabins were probably slave quarters. There was no sign of human occupancy, but, over the door, outlined in black, was a flag. And it was not an old worn flag. It was new and bright red, with a blue cross and three white stars in each arm of the cross.

The rest of the island was densely covered with vegetation, right down to the water. I passed the telescope to Carl. "It's a Confederate battle flag," he said.

"Lemme see," said Rufus. He took a long look through the telescope. "Dat ain't just any Confederate battle flag."

When he passed the instrument back to me his hands shook. "Dat dere is the flag of old General Forrest. I told you this was a bad place."

We had drifted to within two hundred yards of the north end of the island. Gunfire erupted from the island. Holmes fell to his knees. "Gentlemen, get down!" he cried.

Rufus, Carl, and I dropped down to the deck. A volley of bullets whistled over our heads and splashed into the water on either side of the boat. Little puffs of gun smoke hung over the island, but our assailants were well-hidden.

Holmes coolly scanned the shore. "Whoever is shooting at us isn't visible, but he's no ghost. Gentlemen, please pull hard. We need to get out of range."

Carl went to his seat and pulled an oar to turn the boat. In my desperate attempt to duck from the bullets, I skimmed the water with my oars and fell backwards.

Carl managed to turn us towards the middle of the river. We were safe, but we were caught in an eddy current. The violent whirlpool spun our craft like a merry-go-round, further and further into the middle of the mighty river. A furious current took us back towards the island where we were greeted by another volley of rifle fire. A bullet smashed into a plank just at the water line of our boat. Instantly water poured in and we sank lower.

I kept rowing as Rufus and Carl tried to plug the bullet hole. Water poured in. Rufus desperately bailed with his hat while Carl cupped his hands and threw water overboard. Despite their best efforts, the boat settled deeper and deeper into the water.

We could not land on the island and the other shore was too far for us to reach before the boat sank. It looked hopeless.

We were down to the gunwales, frantically bailing with our cupped hands and hats when a low mournful wail rang in our ears. A steamboat was coming our way, a lovely grand vessel traveling upriver at a great speed. Her stern wheel chunked away; black smoke and sparks flew from her twin stacks into the rapidly darkening night.

She did not slow as we waved and shouted. No one on board saw us. To make matters worse, it appeared as if she was going to blindly ram our sinking vessel. Rufus and Carl pulled furiously on their oars. We narrowly escaped being rammed, but the boat had filled with water.

"I cain't swim!" Rufus shouted.

"Hang on to the boat!" I shouted.

Suddenly, from behind the steamer, a small boat rowed by two powerful deckhands came our way. With extraordinary timing they arrived just as our boat was about to sink beneath the waves of Old Muddy. Our poor cockle shell was just barely afloat when our rescuers pulled us onto their little skiff and brought us to the steamer.

Within minutes, we were safely aboard the steamboat, *Natchez*, which was bound from Vicksburg to Memphis. The crew escorted us, dripping wet, through the grand ballroom, with a band and dancing couples, to the officer's quarters.

In all of America, I never saw anything as grand as that Mississippi River steamboat. The gilded decorations, gorgeous furniture, oil paintings, splendid food, abundant drinks, and hand-carved gambling tables took my breath away. She was a glorious embodiment of this young nation. Bold. Brash. Full of steam and power and energy.

Maybe it was our narrow escape from danger that filled us with a certain euphoria, or maybe it was the hot New Orleans coffee fortified with some sort of sweet, syrupy fluid that they served us as we were wrapped in warm blankets. Either way, it was as if we were snatched out of hell and carried into a heavenly abode. I will never forget those several glorious hours we spent on the *Natchez*.

By the time we docked in Memphis we were dry and warm. The tobacco for Holmes's meerschaum pipe was a soggy mess. People often wonder why doctors are so addicted to this vile weed, but they need only endure the stench of an anatomy laboratory to understand.

"I would be happy to fetch pipe tobacco and pick up an El Perfecto cigar for myself," Carl said, with his usual good nature.

"Carl, I appreciate the offer, but it's getting late. You and Arthur should get some rest."

"I don't mind and would enjoy stopping by Angie's for a hot bowl of stew," said Carl.

"Do you want stew or that little blonde?" I teased.

Carl laughed, "The stew."

"Only if Arthur goes with you."

"This has been a most eventful day. I am exhausted and feel I must record everything in my diary before going to sleep," I insisted.

"I don't mind going alone. I'll only be an hour. I'll run to the tobacconist and then Angie's and be at the hotel in no time."

"No Carl, it isn't safe," Holmes said.

Carl immediately left us.

"Doyle, Rufus, follow him. It too dangerous for any of you to be out alone. I will go to the hotel," Holmes said.

Carl had a good lead; we searched the streets and alleyways. He was nowhere to be found. We went to the tobacco shop. It was closed. A loud party was in progress at Angie's. I slipped around to the back door. "I ain't seen hide nor hair of Mister Carl," Ma said.

We gave up and went back to the hotel. Carl had not appeared, but Holmes was waiting in the lobby, a letter in hand.

My Dearest Mr. Holmes,

My carriage will meet you at the hotel nine a.m., tomorrow. The operation we discussed will take place at noon, when there is the best light. I look forward to seeing you then and thank you for your assistance in advance.

Your Most Humble and Obedient Servant,
The Reverend Henry Ward Beecher

7 December, 1878

Holmes, in the lobby paced back and forth, empty pipe in hand. "They have taken Carl. The police have no interest, so, we can only hope the Reverend Beecher will lead us to him."

He arrived promptly at nine. To my surprise, Rebecca was with the minister. We settled ourselves on the opposite seat, leaving room for Rufus who carried the instrument case.

"Is his presence necessary?" Beecher asked.

"Mr. Freeman is studying to be a physician and is an important member of the surgical team. Your operation cannot proceed without him," Holmes replied.

Rebecca's did not meet my gaze. "Jimmy is almost back to his normal self," she murmured.

"That's good. Why are you here?" I murmured.

"I shall nurse the Reverend Beecher after his operation Where is your friend, Carl."

"I see," I turned from her and gazed out the window. "He's gone missing," I said.

"Oh, I am so sorry. I had hoped to see him again."

We galloped in a southerly direction, past fields left fallow for the winter, then through dense woodland and swamps and stopped by a trail that led through a desolate, forbidding swamp.

Two silent men followed us on horseback. They and our driver held Winchester rifles. One man led the way on the trail beneath dark, low-hanging clouds. The rain started with a drizzle, but quickly became a downpour before we reached the waiting steam launch. We huddled in the shelter of the small deckhouse as we chugged downstream past ancient trees hung with a greyish moss. I moved as close as possible to Rebecca, who was hunched in a corner.

Our vessel touched ground, and, while we were balancing on a narrow gangplank that ended in a muddy path, a great flash of lightning revealed the scarlet house and surrounding cabins on top of the small hill. We were on the back side of the island. The back water continued around the southern edge to join the Mississippi.

Our silent guards cradled new Winchester rifles in the crooks of their arms. "Why are you armed?" Holmes asked.

"Damned alligators and rattlesnakes in these swamps," one replied, as he spit a stream of tobacco juice.

I spotted a crumpled, soggy El Perfecto cigar in the weeds alongside our muddy path. Carl must have come this way. He was still alive! A wild chattering, howling, and crying came from the old plantation house. It was an eerie, inhuman sound. The rogue at the head of our column bought his rifle to his shoulder and scanned the trees on either side of the path.

Rufus, for all his superstitions, seemed the least concerned about our surroundings. He proudly carried the instrument case at the head of our dreary column. Holmes remained silent but paced on, with his usual agile quick steps.

Reverend Beecher slipped on a stone, and went down. Rebecca helped him to his feet and on we went.

The howling and chattering grew louder and now I could see the askew columns and the rotting veranda of the old plantation house. One of our keepers shifted his Winchester and, with a large key, unlocked the front door beneath the painted battle flag. We stepped into a long corridor containing odd pieces of once-elegant furniture. It ran the length of the front of the house, and by the light of oil lamps I identified four doors leading off the corridor. The chattering and crying, which had ceased when we entered the corridor, started again, this time with greater intensity and a note of madness and anger.

To my amazement, the door to our left opened into a clean whitewashed room. Rain beat against a skylight that admitted light the color of cast iron. Oil lamps relieved the gloom.

There was a plain wooden operating table in the center of the room beneath the skylight. Shelves filled with medical supplies lined the walls. Next to the operating table was a small table with a wash basin, soap, and towels. The room was heated by an old-fashioned open fireplace.

My eyes swept across what was to be our operating room. In addition to the entrance, there was another closed door. Did it lead to another room or to the outside? A tall, stooped woman clad in the white floor-length dress of a proper operating room sister was in charge. A bonnet pulled low obscured her hair and features. Upon our arrival, she ceased stacking linen on a shelf and half turned with a folded towel over her right hand.

"The table is freshly scrubbed and prepared for the Reverend Beecher. You may place the instruments there." She pointed to another table covered with a white sheet. "I trust everything is satisfactory."

Holmes eyed the room and the arrangements. "Everything is well-organized, but where is the Reverend Beecher's physician?"

"Dr. Droussard will be here after he secures the glandular material."

Rufus placed the instrument case on the edge of the table. The minister, holding Rebecca's arm, tottered into the operating room, removed his coat and shirt and stretched out on the table.

"Prepare both arms, please. The doctor may implant two glands," said the nurse.

Rufus soaked the instruments in carbolic and Rebecca, at Holmes' instructions, swabbed both of the Reverend Beecher's arms with the antiseptic.

Holmes made no effort to sooth or reassure Beecher. His interest in the operation was purely scientific.

I prepared the anesthetic, but little ether would be required, since the incision was only skin deep. Miss Yates arranged the instruments on a clean towel. As the room quieted, a low moan and a gurgling sound came from the back room. This was a human sound. The Reverend was breathing quietly, and the others were concentrating on our patient. I slowly inched open the door.

Suddenly, large, rough, powerful hands grabbed me by the shoulders and dragged me into the next room. I could not cry out. In the struggle, I felt a stab to my right buttock and immediately, lost voluntary motion, first in my legs, then my arms. The drug, curare had me in its hold. I was still perfectly aware of my surroundings, with unimpaired vision and hearing. However, when they roughly placed me on a table, I realized I was no longer able to hold up my head and could not breathe. I remembered Holmes' advice to breathe with the diaphragm, the muscle that separates the abdomen from the chest cavity. When death seemed imminent, a minute amount of air entered my lungs. The diaphragm was working.

The low moan and gurgling was close by. My assailants had let my head turn to one side. I looked upon a dreadful scene. Blood dripped from an adjoining table where Carl, naked from the waist up and strapped to a table. A gowned, hooded figure held his head while another dissected with knife and forceps deep into a bloody hole in his neck.

The paralyzing drug that they had given us both still had me in its hold, but Carl squirmed as they probed his neck in an attempt to remove his thyroid gland.

Suddenly, Carl jerked and his eyes rolled towards me with a startled look of recognition.

I was immobilized and could not help him. The surgeon with painstaking slowness dissected through the nerves, blood vessels and muscles of Carl's neck.

There was a steady drip of blood, and occasionally a crimson spray when the sharp knife cut through an artery.

I could not force even the merest twitch of movement but felt only constant suffocation.

The high-pitched chattering increased along with banging on a side door. I drifted in and out of consciousness while the operation on Carl proceeded step by agonizing step. I had no sensation of the passage of time, but concentrated on each shallow breath. Carl's moans and gurgling respirations became weaker until, with one final gasp, his beseeching eyes turned to me. *"Kill me. Now. Please,"* they seemed to plead.

His life's blood drained out onto the floor and I knew he was at death's door. My foggy, oxygen-starved brain understood. They were not implanting glands into the Reverend Beecher from animals, but from human beings. They had kidnapped Carl to implant his thyroid into the Reverend.

The nurse had said they would implant two glands. I was the next subject.

Rough hands straightened my body into a supine position and tilted my head backwards to expose the flesh of my neck to the surgeon's knife.

The memory of the scene that followed is both a confused blur and a vivid nightmare.

The chattering increased to a frenzied howl, and the door on the opposite side of the room swung open. A horde of screeching and howling monkeys flew out through the door and descended on the hooded figures ripping, clawing, and biting.

The surgeon and the medical assistant slashed at the animals with surgical knives, but the frenzied animals tore away their hoods and robes and clawed their flesh into bloody strips. The surgeon, Emilie Droussard covered her face but the animals ripped her skin and bit deep into her neck, chest, and head.

Her blood mingled with Carl's. She struggled against the mad onslaught until, mercifully for her, she swooned.

One large, fierce monkey fastened on to the back of her assistant who I now realized was the tobacco-spitting man with the Winchester rifle who had walked us to the scarlet house.

The man beat the animal with his bare hands and struck it with the butt of his rifle, but to no avail. Two monkeys shredded his face with their razor-sharp teeth.

As if possessed by demons, the ferocious monkeys tore his eyes from their sockets. He emitted an unholy scream and sunk, lifeless, to the floor.

Throughout this ghastly uproar, I fully expected the monkeys to attack me and Carl. We were helpless and the next victims.

A monkey even jumped onto my chest, but, instead of ripping me to pieces, to my amazement, it merely sniffed and leaped away.

Suddenly, the once-ferocious monkeys became docile as family pets and scampered about, lapping up human blood.

Two of the animals leaped up on to the surgical table, sniffed Carl, and made sad, mewing sounds. Carl stirred. He was alive but his chest hardly moved.

It all made sense when I dimly remembered surgical scars on the monkeys. They had been subject to dreadful experiments and were taking revenge on their tormenters.

Suddenly, the room went grey, then black. Holmes later said my eyes were wide open, but I was unconscious when he and Rebecca burst into the room.

They had heard the ruckus and, fortunately, arrived just in time. Rebecca thought I was dead and, with quick thinking, grabbed the bellows from the fireplace. "Mr. Holmes he isn't breathing!" she shouted.

Holmes pumped air into my lungs.

At the first twinge of returning muscle activity, I weakly brushed the wooden nozzle away from my mouth, coughed, spluttered, and took a deep breath. "Save Carl," I said.

Poor Carl was near the end of his life. He needed a miracle.

"He has a faint pulse!" Holmes shouted. "Miss Yates, the instruments."

Rebecca snatched up clamps, needles, and thread. In the merest twinkling of an eye, Holmes sutured bleeding arteries and veins. I groggily wondered at his many skills. The fellow could be a great surgeon if he chose to focus on one area of expertise.

In the midst of the frantic efforts to stitch the wound, Carl had stopped breathing. Holmes snatched up the bellows and pumped air into his lungs until Carl took a weak breath, coughed, sputtered, and came back to life.

(I do not remember a great deal about my rescue. Therefore, I must admit that the details as written were related to me by Rebecca after these events took place. She also told of the events as they transpired in the adjoining room of the scarlet house in the few minutes before my rescue. Ergo, the following text is his tale as they related it to me after it occurred.)

Sherlock Holmes was focused on the operation, dubious, yet excited about, the possibilities of a great scientific breakthrough. Lister's antiseptic technique made it possible to remove or repair diseased organs. If this operation succeeded, organ implantation could become a reality.

Before leaving I had administered sufficient ether and the nursing sister indicated the organ was nearly ready in the adjacent room. When Holmes realized I was missing, he put down the scalpel and demanded to know my whereabouts. The nursing sister insisted that he continue with the operation. He expressed concern and adamantly refused until she revealed my whereabouts. Holmes threatened her with the surgical knife but the nursing sister was no woman. In the scuffle, her gown came loose to reveal a hook on her right arm. "She" was Captain Spencer or, as he is better known, Captain Hook.

The villain jumped away, seized Rebecca just beneath her jaw with his terribly sharp hook and, with his good hand, pulled a long-barreled revolver. His face was contorted with rage, and he had the strength of a mad man.

Holmes immediately poised the scalpel over Beecher's chest.

"Damn you! I shall plunge this knife into his heart. Release the girl."

Although Spencer was far gone into madness, Rufus flung himself at the Captain. The man fired his pistol, but his aim was poor. The bullet grazed Rufus on the side of his chest. The ragged wound was bloody and painful, but not lethal.

Just before he collapsed, Rufus seized the weapon. Thankfully, the open instrument case was close at hand. Holmes reached into the secret niche and withdrew the Bull Dog revolver.

His first shot splintered the doorway. He aimed again, but Hook used Rebecca as a shield, so he lowered the gun.

(Here, Miss Yates took up the narrative. She spoke in a low, almost inaudible voice, while twisting a handkerchief. She was clearly under great emotional strain as she spoke, but I felt it important to convey her story in order to complete this narrative.)

It all happened so fast. He dragged me backwards and said he would kill me if Holmes didn't continue the operation. I felt helpless and terrified as the cold metal of his hook dug into my throat.

With his last ounce of strength, heroic Rufus pushed him off balance and took his gun. When Holmes fired, I wrenched free. Hook fled down the corridor, tearing off the dress as he ran. In his flight, he knocked over an oil lamp. Oil spilled and burst into flames. The fire spread through the old furniture and dry wood. He reached the front door and disappeared. "Down with tyrants!" he screamed.

(Holmes took up the narrative.)

When I reached Rebecca, the corridor was already filled with black smoke and flames were licking at the walls. Captain Hook had disappeared, but a door at the end of the hall opened and a man holding a rifle and a whip stepped out.

When I fired, he ran and disappeared around the corner, apparently following Captain Hook into the approaching night.

To my amazement and utter horror, a pack of shrieking monkeys emerged from the door and ran through the flames and smoke. They ignored us and scampered out of the house.

After I had seen to Rebecca and staunched the bleeding from Rufus's chest, I then proceeded to help you and Carl.

(I shall now continue the narrative from my own perspective.)

As Carl and I recovered, Holmes and Rebecca dragged Rufus into our "operating room." They then pulled the Reverend Beecher from the approaching flames. He was still recovering from the anaesthetic. They slammed the door behind them, but the smoke poured in through the cracks around the doorstop.

Flames were rapidly consuming the house, smoke was filling our room, and we could not see a way out. A quick inspection of the 'operating room' revealed the windows were barred on the outside and there was no other door.

We considered making a run through the flames to an exit, but the floorboards collapsed. We seemed destined to die of asphyxiation in this ghastly room in this gruesome scarlet house.

Emilie Droussard stirred. "Mr. Holmes, . . . Please . . ." She slowly raised her bloody arm and pointed to a shelf.

Holmes knelt by her side and listened to her nearly inaudible voice "It was a mad dream . . . My casebook . . . Take it. You will see . . ."

Her arm fell back and her eyes closed. She made a deep shuddering sigh. Her eyes fluttered open, "If only . . . The implant..."

Her voice drifted off, and then her eyes brightened for an instant. "To hays . . . Below the tomb!"

She said nothing more, but took another raspy breath. Her eyes went dim with the blank emptiness of death. Holmes slipped her leather-bound notebook into his coat pocket.

Rufus groaned and smoke continued to fill the room, Rebecca slumped and fell to the floor. She struck the hard wooden floorboards with a loud *FWUNK*. I was badly shaken, but knelt by her side, fanning her face and massaging her hands. I coughed. The smoke was thick. We were lost.

"Doyle, there was a hollow sound when Rebecca hit the floor? Inspect the floorboards!" Holmes yelled.

I ran my hands along the floorboards but noticed nothing unusual until my hand struck upon something cold and metallic. Brass. There was a round, tarnished brass door-pull set deeply into a plank in the floorboards. It was a trapdoor handle.

It was a trapdoor that led to a flight of stairs, then into a cavernous basement dug out of the earth and lined by crude bricks. Like priest-holes in old English homes, many pre-Civil War homes in America had trapdoors that led to tunnels. We were saved, thanks to Sherlock Holmes and his great powers of observation.

I supported Rufus while we made our way down wet, moss-covered wooden stairs into the dank subterranean room. The Reverend Beecher, now fully recovered from the ether, followed us. Carl struggled to his feet, but he collapsed.

Rebecca, poor, sweet Rebecca helped Carl to his feet and down the stairs of the tunnel.

Once everybody was safely below the ground, I slammed the trapdoor against the dense smoke and breathed a sigh of relief. Holmes lowered Rufus to the earthen floor. I struck a lucifer.

By the flickering yellow light, we made out dozens of wooden crates labeled U.S. ARMORY, WINCHESTER CALIBRE

.45-70 RIFLES. Were these the guns stolen from an arsenal in Illinois? I had no time to ponder the question. It was pitch dark when my match went out.

I used up all but one match while exploring to find an exit. There was nothing. I pulled slivers of wood from a crate and, with my last match, created a makeshift torch.

I held the burning slivers high and explored more until I felt a slight draft of fresh air from a side tunnel leading down and away from the crude basement.

"Follow me." I went ahead with the dim torch. Our motley parade trudged in the dark towards the draft of fresh air. Rats scurried away and we brushed aside spider webs.

We had been in the tunnel no more than a few minutes when a terrific explosion shook the earth. Bricks flew from the walls and all around us the tunnel began to collapse.

"My God, there must have been enough powder and ammunition there for a small army," said Holmes "Hurry, before we are buried alive."

We hastened on until a speck of light appeared ahead in the tunnel. In a moment, we emerged only a few yards from the big river. The tunnel entrance was well-hidden by trees and foliage. Muddy footprints in a worn trail leading to a crude landing indicated recent use.

I searched, but the steam launch that had brought us here was gone, most likely taken by Captain Hook and his rifle-toting crony.

Flames and dense smoke still shot skyward from the old scarlet plantation house and rapidly spread to the cabins. The house collapsed into a veritable crematorium for Emilie Droussard and her accomplices. Meanwhile, the storm moved on, leaving a yellow haze that marked the sun setting across the great river.

About an hour later, a side-wheeler packet boat pushing a flat-bottomed barge had paused in mid-river, evidently to watch the spectacular pyrotechnics. We shouted and waved. Holmes fired three quick shots from the Bull Dog revolver.

The Reverend Beecher finally proved of some value when he shouted in his best stentorian voice. "HELP! HELP! We have injured men here!"

She was the *Lucy B*, an elderly tug pushing a barge upriver. Her great wheel churned mud, but she edged close enough to our landing for husky black deckhands to help us aboard.

We huddled among bales of cotton, trying to make Carl and Rufus comfortable. Carl had lost a lot of blood and had used all of his remaining energy to get through the tunnel. He was pale and weak as he rested on the cotton bales.

Rufus coughed and spit blood as if the bullet had grazed his lung. More blood oozed from his chest wound. Fortunately, the bullet had entered his lower chest and exited from his side. Holmes swabbed his wounds with carbolic and applied a tight bandage torn from his shirt.

Rebecca, now fully revived took over his care with great tenderness. The five of us huddled together and sat away from the Reverend Beecher. The old fellow was angry that we had not implanted the thyroid gland. He was still convinced the operation would have made him into a new man. Even now, he could not believe that his doctor was a fraud.

We reached the Memphis landing a few hours later and, with difficulty, roused a drayman and his wagon.

With my energy somewhat restored by the fresh air, I went ahead and informed the Burks of our plight. They were more than willing to take in my injured companions and tend to their needs. Upon arrival at the Burks' house, Rebecca, Dr. Bell, and I carried Rufus and then Carl into the home of the friendly Quakers.

Rebecca shook her red curls. "I shall have nothing more to do with the Reverend Beecher. Please, Mrs. Burk, I have a little money and will pay if you can let my ward, Jimmy, stay with you for a few days while I care for these two injured men." Her eyes flashed with an emotion that I had never witnessed in the girl.

"Of course, dear, you may stay as long as you wish."

Sherlock Holmes and I retired to the hotel where I am once again at my desk with pencil and paper recording the events of this incredible day. I am at this moment reading out loud to Holmes who corrected some of my observations. To the best of my memory it is all true. I owe my life to this enigmatic, brilliant man. Someday, I shall immortalize him with my writing.

8 December, 1878

In the morning, after a restless night, Holmes and I picked up Jimmy from the Paynes' mansion and delivered him to the Burks' house.

"What about the Reverend. Beecher," I asked.

"You need not worry about that scoundrel. The sly old dog slithered back to Brooklyn on the first train. The old fraud tried to swear me to secrecy before he left and said he would pray for us." Holmes said with a dry laugh.

We brought young Jimmy to the Burks' home. Rufus and Carl were on makeshift pallets in our old lean-to bedroom. Their wounds were clean, but both were in pain. When we arrived with Jimmy, Miss Yates was administering laudanum to Carl. My friend gazed at her with love-smitten eyes. She caressed his hand and returned his loving gaze. Was it possible? Had they fallen in love overnight?

Rebecca rose, hugged little Jimmy and gave me a mere glance. "Mrs. Burk will allow me to stay as long as it takes to restore Carl and Rufus to health," said she. She smiled warmly as she spoke. In that moment, a spark flashed between Rebecca and Carl, and I knew that they had taken a fancy to each other.

Despite all my efforts to woo her, she had instead fallen for my friend from Wisconsin. I felt green-eyed jealousy. Our star-crossed love was not to be. Even with a broken heart, I would wish them well. She was the pretty nurse that Carl longed for. Perhaps the prophecy of Mrs. Burk's tea leaves was correct and marrying her would have upset my Maw. My scientific mind would not accept the occult, but perhaps there are unknown mysteries.

We were in Mrs. Burk's kitchen, drinking coffee. Holmes lit up his pipe. "The scoundrel Hook is still at large," he said.

"Is he still a threat," I asked.

"Do you remember Emilie Droussard's dying words?"

174

"Something about 'to hays below the tomb.'"

Rufus weakly lifted his head from the pallet. "Sir, dey's only one tomb important to those damn Confederates. The good folks up North buried Mister Lincoln in a fine tomb in Springfield, Illinois."

"They might steal the body, to further their cause. Doyle, let us take a walk. The fresh air might help," Holmes said.

It was a sunny, fine day with just a bit of a breeze. We strolled to the Peabody for lunch, and as is his habit, Holmes stopped in the lobby to check the newspapers.

"My God. Doyle, according to this article, President Rutherford B. Hayes is travelling through the Midwest to Kansas, and back through Springfield, Illinois. The President was to end his tour with a final address at Lincoln's tomb at four o'clock in the afternoon on the ninth day of December.

I gasped. "That was her message. Not to hays, but to Rutherford B. HAYES."

"Aye and BELOW the tomb. President Hayes will be delivering a speech on the balustrade BELOW the obelisk marking Lincoln's tomb, and he very well might share Lincoln's fate if we do not intercede," said Holmes.

TOMORROW! The President was going to be in Springfield in one day. We had to get there if we were to stop something awful from happening.

"Get a cab! We must warn Mr. Duncan at once!" Holmes shouted.

I hailed the first cab. Holmes offered the driver a gold eagle to reach the central depot and the telegraph office within five minutes. The driver whipped his horse to a furious gallop. Four minutes later we reached the depot.

Holmes presented his scribbled message to the operator, an obese gentleman with a flowing white beard dotted with brown dribbles of tobacco juice.

"Please send this urgent message to Mr. Angus Duncan in Chicago," Holmes said. The message read: *Alert the Pinkertons. Captain Spencer plans to assassinate the president tomorrow at Lincoln's tomb at four o'clock in the afternoon. Must be stopped.*

The operator chewed his gob of tobacco while reading the message, paused for a moment, then aimed a stream of brown spit at Holmes polished boot. "You damn Yankees have done enough damage."

"I am a subject of her British majesty. Not a Yankee."

"If you ain't Southern, you're a damn Yankee in my book. I would be damned to hell before I send this message for you, even if I could. Big ice storm up North, all lines are down, bridges washed out, ain't even no trains runnin'."

"Please route the message to another line. I shall pay you in gold," said Holmes.

"Hell, no."

"I shall call the police."

"Go ahead. They locked up the last carpetbagger who came into town. Sure they would be happy to lock you up, too."

The operator was correct. No trains were running north. We consulted the station map. "It is over three hundred miles to Springfield. If we ride day and night, we can make it in time."

"Horses won't be able to get us there in time. Do you have any other ideas?" I said

"Yes, we ride horseback to Cairo, Illinois and catch a train."

We obtained two good horses and saddles and immediately set out at a gallop on the only road heading north. The first fifteen miles sped by, but our horses were tiring and my backside was already sore as a boil.

We were on the outskirts of a small town when we spied a crowd of men, lads, and women around an open field. As we drew closer we saw a hot air balloon being inflated.

"Whoa!" Holmes shouted. "This demands investigation."

A portly man in a set of white overalls paced in front of the balloon on jerky steps while wringing his hands. "Ladies and Gents. Just one dollar a person for a full twenty-five-minute ride in the world's largest hot air balloon . . . Boys, be the first to tell your friends you kissed your girl while five-hundred feet in the air."

A few young fellows scuffed their feet and looked interested, but no one opened their wallets. A wicker basket was connected to the balloon that was tethered to the ground with ropes. Above the basket, flames from a metal tank heated the air that inflated the balloon.

"Sir, can your balloon go as far as Springfield, Illinois?" Holmes asked.

"Well, well, well . . . Lookee here, lookee here . . . Hear that there accent, folks? Yes, they come all the way from England to ride Oscar's world famous balloon."

"I am from Scotland, not England," said I.

"Either way, you came to the right place, gents. Yes, sir, it is your lucky day." He held a finger to the wind. "If this south wind holds, she could probably take you all the way back home to Scotland."

"And the fee, sir?" Holmes asked.

"Since you gentlemen came all this way; I'll give you a special discount. Remember, this is the world's largest balloon and a once-in-a-lifetime opportunity. Take a ride! Take a death-defying ride and make history!" he said, as much to the crowd as to us.

"The fee, sir?"

"Because the British have been such great friends to these here Colonies and you are so beloved, I shall give a special fee, reserved customarily for family members. And gents, this fee will be a special offer, a never-to-be-repeated price. A mere one hundred dollars."

"We shall give you the horses and saddles now, and eighty if you can get us there by three o'clock to-morrow."

"DEAL. You gents drive a hard bargain. And please do not tell another soul about this special rate that I only give to friends from across the pond in merry old England." He extended his hand and shook Holmes hand. "The name's Oscar. Oscar Blithe. My balloon is named *Blithe Spirit*. Now, climb in the basket and off we go."

We introduced ourselves and climbed in. "Make haste, sir. We have no time to lose, and need to go as soon as possible," I urged.

"As you wish. We'll be off in a moment. Just need to turn up the heat."

The balloon itself was constructed of panels of red, white, and blue silk. The gas tank, suspended just within reach above the basket, was equipped with a valve to control the flow of gas, and a flint and steel igniter that made a spark when the operator pulled a string.

After we crowded into the basket Mr. Blithe opened a valve. Blue flames shot upward sending hot air into the balloon. The great silken bag inflated and tugged at its mooring line. "Let her go!" Oscar shouted.

We hauled in the ropes and we were up and away.

When we were high over the tree tops, Oscar shut off the gas and we sailed through the sky in absolute silence. It was so perfectly peaceful; unlike anything I had known. I felt tension and worry draining away. Happily, I had brought my diary and a pencil with me so I could record the experience.

I was calm and tranquil for the first time in many days. The sighing wind and clear skies were a balm to my soul. It was utter serenity — that is until Oscar broke into my thoughts.

"You folks are in for a real treat. It's a clear sunny day and you can see forever. We're following the river to Cairo. Then, if the wind holds, we will strike a compass course to Springfield." Oscar stated this with so much enthusiasm that I was convinced we would reach Springfield in plenty of time.

At one point, Oscar gave up on his travelogue and began fussing with the gas burner. My gaze rested upon the great river, which twisted and turned for miles and miles like an endless serpent. There were sandbars, shores lined with greeny-grey trees, and a few villages hugging the river banks. Steamboats glided along, belching clouds of dense black smoke.

I scarcely had words to describe the magnificence of this land, which made me wonder if I could ever really be a good enough writer to share my adventures with the world.

This was the first time I truly had the opportunity to study Sherlock Holmes in repose. He had removed his great cape and the wool hat with earflaps that so effectively repels the icy, whistling winds and drenching rains of our climate. His eyes were closed against the sun and he folded his hands over chest. I could not help but sketch his aquiline profile and jutting jaw to fasten that moment in my memory.

The wind was in less force, which meant our speed diminished. Holmes came instantly awake, reached for his great curved pipe, tamped in tobacco, lit up and watched the smoke drift skyward.

"Mr. Blithe, we are slowing. If you please, make more speed." he asked.

"I'll give her some more gas. We'll get a better wind if we go higher up," Mr. Blithe said.

He opened the valve and pulled the igniter string again. Immediately, a blue flame roared out of the tank and the balloon lifted higher and then even higher.

We flew along as fast as a railway train, but Oscar said we were going no more than twenty-five miles an hour. Either way, I figured that we were going more than fast enough to get us to Springfield in time.

Riding in the balloon was a welcome, tranquil experience and a great relief after being shot at in Chicago, nearly hanged by the James Gang, almost drowned, poisoned by curare, scared half to death by vengeance-seeking monkeys, and losing Rebecca.

However, the placidity was occasionally broken by our balloonist. As we passed over a sizable village, farm, or town, Oscar waved and yelled "hallo!" to folks gathered below. The people looked upward as if hearing a voice from heaven and then waved and hollered back. From our vantage point, they were as small as dolls. Oscar was a lively fellow and had evidently entertained guests before.

"Would you fellows care for a little snack or drink of homemade hooch?"

Oscar hoisted a jug and glugged down a half a cup of raw hooch.

"English balloonists serve champagne," said Holmes.

I wolfed down a half-loaf of hard black bread and a moldy hunk of cheddar cheese. I even took a sip of Oscar's homebrew. Holmes refused the jug but took a nip from the small green bottle of laudanum. "Mr. Blithe, we must not get behind our schedule. Please, make haste."

"Have no worries, my friends. I will have you in Springfield within the hour," Oscar responded.

Except for the wind and the occasional roar of the gas flame, it was once again tranquil. I rushed to write down my final thoughts because, surely, our adventure was soon to be over. Sadly, too, all was over with Rebecca. I searched for a word that could help me move on and the one that came to mind was *exorcise*. Yes, I would erase her from my thoughts and remember this grand landscape.

While I was writing we passed over a lake. With no warning a whirlwind struck the balloon. Suddenly, our basket was swinging madly, like a pendulum. I was forced to put aside my pencil and cling to a rope for dear life. The basket tipped, made a great splintering noise, and spun like a top. I was certain we would fall to our death. Holmes although deathly pale calmly puffed his pipe.

Oscar remained his jovial self. "Ain't nothin', boys. Just warm air rising from that lake down under. Old *Blithe Spirit* has seen worse than this. Have some more whisky."

I held tight and felt the bread, cheese, and homebrew burn the back of my throat. I swallowed and tried not to throw up. We must have been a thousand feet high. The setting sun was almost covered by streaky white clouds. There were more ominous clouds ahead, and the wind was changing fast.

"Mr. Blithe, damn all, we are veering too far to the east. You must keep us on course to Springfield!" Holmes shouted.

Oscar shielded his eyes. "Yep, that there hill should be on our left. We are a might off course."

"How can that be? You are supposed to steer this contraption and keep us on course!"

"Well, sir, that is the thing with hot air balloons. They ain't like a horse and buggy. You can't just keep 'em right on course, especially if God don't blow wind in the right direction."

"You said you would get us to Springfield."

"Well, sir, God's the pilot and we just go along for the ride. Ain't nothin' me or you or nobody else can do about it."

"And you chose not to mention this until now."

"Yes, sir. I reckoned that you already knew that, but maybe I mighta been wrong."

"Sir, our British balloonists regularly stay on course across the English Channel," said Holmes.

"This ain't no damn channel," Oscar replied.

Dark clouds crowded the horizon, dusk fell, and, suddenly, our blissful day turned ominous and cold. Holmes pulled his cape coat tighter, and I wished I had mother's wool scarf.

Oscar took a long drink. "She will go down when the air in the balloon gets colder. Don't you worry none. Things are gonna be just fine. Who knows? We might even land within a few hundred miles of Springfield."

I grabbed my head in disgust. We did drop down a ways, but, then, in the dark, it was hard knowing if we were high enough to clear the trees. We swooped over a small town and, judging from the lights, we were barely over the rooftops.

"Dang, we ain't high enough, need more hot air. I'll light her up," Oscar said.

He pulled the string. The flint and steel made a spark, but no flame.

"Damn, we must be outta gas. Probably shoulda checked that out before we lifted off."

Holmes sighed. "That would have been a good idea."

Oscar snapped the flint and pounded on the gas tank, but there was no flame. We dropped lower and lower, and, suddenly, I saw two glittery rivers just ahead. Oscar hopped on one foot, then the other.

"Boys, I got good news for you. That there first river's the Mississippi and the second's the Ohio, which means that if we can clear the first and land before we hit the second, we are as good as gold."

"If?"

"Yes, sir. You see, right there between the two is the town of Cairo, Illinois. Cairo's perfect. From there, you'll easily catch a train to Springfield. So, all I gotta do is figure out how to land this thing now and make sure we don't sink in either of them there big rivers."

"You don't know how to land?" asked Dr. Bell.

"I was just joking. Of course I do. I mean . . . I just ain't never landed in the dark, ain't got that much experience. Always figured landing at night was too dangerous."

"Great God in Heaven, preserve us," I groaned.

A long pregnant silence hung like an ominous cloud over us. We barely breathed as we silently floated over the Mississippi. The murky water rolled on with little waves and whitecaps. Even if we landed in the water, our basket might float, but we would surely freeze.

A sudden puff of wind, pushed us to the far bank of that massive brown river and we floated over a glade of trees. "Now! Now! Now! Cut loose those sandbags if you don't want to drown in the Ohio!" Oscar shouted.

I opened a penknife and, with a quick slash, cut the ropes. Two sandbags fell away. We rose a few feet before settling down again. For a frightful moment, the basket touched water. Oscar cut loose two more bags. We rose twenty feet or so and glided across the Ohio River.

The wind picked up speed. We whirled through the gathering darkness with tree branches dragging at the basket. An updraft gave us another bounce for a moment, and we sailed on into the night.

I was down on the floor of the basket when Holmes fell across my legs.

"Mr. Blithe, get this thing under control!" he shouted.

There was another jolt and we dragged and bumped against tree branches. "Ain't nothing left to do. I done tried everything, but I ain't got the experience. My cousin, Lester, crashed and died in this very same basket just a month ago. Nobody in the family wanted it, so I inherited the balloon, basket, and a month's supply of gas." Oscar said.

I looked heavenward, but, instead of sky, saw only the crazy balloon fluttering like a half-empty sac. I hardly remember the next few seconds. Holmes struggled, to his feet, then fell in a heap. Oscar covered his face. "Hang on! She's gonna hit!" he shouted.

Our basket with the collapsed balloon crashed down, down through the branches of a giant tree. The gas tank struck Oscar, then we splintered wood and crashed through a roof.

The basket split in half. Oscar went flying and landed on his back, cuddling his jug like a baby. Holmes was nowhere to be seen. I was down on all fours amidst a furious flutter of wings and angry squawking. I wiped feathers out of my eyes and, when my head cleared, heard angry barking, snarling and a boy's voice in an excited shout. "PAW! PAW! THEY'S THIEVES IN THE HEN HOUSE. GIT THE GUN!"

A light went on in a farm house not thirty feet away and the back door opened. I saw an older woman who wore a long white nightgown and carried a lantern. A skinny old fellow stood in the doorway, raised a long gun, and *BOOM*!

Oscar had struggled to his feet and raised the jug, which shattered in a charge of birdshot. More pellets rattled on the chicken coop and made tree leaves go a-flutter. The shot further enraged a great snarling mastiff with bared teeth who tugged at a rusty chain.

The old fellow, his nightshirt fluttering at his knees, rammed home another charge. We were caught in the light.

I was still down, batting away a huge rooster, when Holmes rose to his full six feet, two inches. His cap was askew. The two bills were over his ears and an earflap covered one eye. With his outstretched arms, his billowing cape looked for all the world like wings.

"Man, do not fire the gun and control the beast. We are not thieves, but poor folk fallen from the heavens."

The old lady went to her knees with hands clasped prayer.

"Oh, blessed Lord, you sent an angel from heaven!"

"Good lady, we shall gladly pay for the damages to your chicken coop." Holmes offered a glittering ten-dollar gold piece.

"Hallelujah, we are saved!" the woman cried. "Is that real gold?"

"From the United States mint," said Holmes.

"Ma, boil up some coffee. Show these folks hospitality."

We crowded into a kitchen with a wood stove and a plank floor. The old lady set a kettle over a crackling fire and crushed coffee beans with a hammer.

I chocked down the foul, bitter brew and, was glad to be alive.

I toyed with my cup. "Mr. Blithe, you promised to deliver us to Springfield."

"I reckon you can get a train in Cairo and be there in no time at all. I dun' pretty good considerin' the circumstances and all, and, on account of you fellers are English I'll reduce the charge to ten dollars. But, don't tell a soul you didn't pay the full price."

"Damn, you scoundrel, we aren't even in Cairo."

The old farmer hitched up his nightshirt and scratched a skinny leg. "If you got another one of them ten dollar pieces, I kin drive you into Cairo in time to catch the train."

"It's a deal." Holmes handed the gold coin to the aged farmer.

We piled the shredded balloon, the basket, and ourselves in wagon drawn by two balky mules and set off through brush and across fields in the direction of Cairo. I drowsed off, but jerked awake when a hoot owl screeched.

It got easier when we came upon wagon tracks that, after a bit, led to a road and the outskirts of Cairo.

The mules ambled on the dirt road past big houses that belonged to steamboat captains and a building that Oscar said was the Customs House — which also served as a post office and courthouse.

There was not a single light or a soul on the streets. Not even a night watchman could be seen. We reached a fallen-down frame building with a porch and rocking chairs that Oscar said was a public house.

"I'm stoppin' right here. You lads go on another block to the train depot. The agent keeps the place warm," the farmer said.

We said our goodbyes and went to the cheerless depot. There was no sign of an agent, but the ancient wood-burning stove had a few glowing embers. We flopped on the floor and dozed off.

9 December, 1878

It was just light, maybe six o'clock in the morning when the Cairo stationmaster kicked my ribs with a hobnail boot. "Damn tramps. Get out of my station," he said.

"We aren't tramps," I said.

"Oh pshaw, you can't fool me. You talk like some foreigner."

Holmes was immediately alert. "We are guests of Angus Duncan who owns the railroad." He pulled out his wallet and waved a fistful of American dollars at the uncouth man. "We demand immediate transport to Springfield, and damn the expense."

"Well, this is a different story. The next train ain't due for another hour. You boys might as well go across the street and have breakfast."

Holmes had toast with jam. I polished off a half-dozen fried eggs, ham, and biscuits with gravy. It cost a dollar. We rushed back to the station but the agent was nowhere to be found. Holmes wrote out a telegram to warn the Pinkertons and added a note for the agent, "Urgent. Send as soon as possible," and left a gold ten-dollar coin.

It was an anxious hour but the unflappable Sherlock Holmes quietly puffed his pipe. At half nine a slow-moving goods train, with a tired wood-fired steam engine pulling two cars, chugged into the station and wheezed to a stop. The name *GLADYS* was painted in red across the boiler.

I hailed the engineer. "Ho, we need immediate transportation to Springfield. It is a matter of life and death. Your president is in danger."

"Ach, now. As surely as my name is Billy O'Toole I'd help you gentlemen, but ya can't fool me with a damn cock and bull story."

Billy O'Toole climbed down off the engine and ran a hand through sparse hair. I recognized a fellow Irishman by his merry eyes and red nose with broken veins. Billy clearly enjoyed a drink.

Holmes took in the situation with a single glance and jingled gold coins.

"Mr. O'Toole, you will be generously rewarded and I shall put in a good word for you with Mr. Angus Duncan who owns the railroad."

"Ah, you are two pretty boys. This is a freight, don't carry no passengers. How do I know you ain't Pinkertons trying to catch me out with a bribe? My old pal, Tommy Jenkins, on the St. Louis line, lost his job when he let his drinking pals ride a freighter. I ain't gonna make the same mistake."

"Mr. O'Toole, consider our money as honest payment for passage, not a bribe. You have my word," said Holmes.

"I wish I could help, but, no, sir. You can't fool me."

"Just one second. The broken blood vessels in your nose might at first appear to be windburn, but I would wager that they are telangiectasia rosacea resulting from your over-reliance on alcohol; further confirmed by the fact that even though your back pocket is empty the dye of the material is worn away in the faint outline of a flask. You drink on the job, and the pork grease under your fingernails and the scent of ham on your sleeves indicate that you are stealing cargo," said Holmes.

"Well, you don't say." Billy hung his head, then came up with a sheepish smile. "Why shucks, if you boys don't mind ridin' old *Gladys* with the freight, come on board and we are on our way. You got two choices, ride with the smoked pork or sit on the grain sacks."

Holmes sniffed. "Those are our only choices?"

"Yep. Now I'll fire her up and go like lightning, but we gotta cross the Big Muddy River."

"Never heard of that river," said I.

"Ain't on no map, but this time of the year she runs pretty fast, and there is so much mud the fish can't see the bait. Trouble is, the only bridge is mighty shaky. Some days, I gotta wait till the water goes down."

"We shall take that risk, sir. Sally forth," Holmes replied.

The bags of grain were a might uncomfortable, but we snuggled under a canvas tarpaulin. It was not so bad. The old train did not go like lightning but, instead, puttered along at a snail's pace. It was bloody hard to be patient and then the train shuddered, clanked, sputtered, and jerked to a stop.

Billy clambered down from the cab and wiped his nose. We joined the little Irishman on the banks of a raging muddy stream. "This here is the Big Muddy River and there is the bridge."

The iron tracks were laid on a slender wooden trestle that trembled with each wave. A tree branch, rolling with the fast current, struck a wood piling. The bridge shook and creaked.

Holmes opened his fine gold watch. "We must hurry on. The President's address starts in four hours. If that telegraph operator sent our message, the Pinkertons might save the President, but they will not know to look for Captain Hook. The entire country may be in dire straits."

"Aye, we are in a dire rush, but will the bridge hold?" I asked.

"*Gladys* is a heavy loaded old bitch, but there's a 50/50 chance we kin make it." Billy twinkled with a crafty smile. "Now boys, let me see the color of your money."

Holmes peeled off ten dollar bills. "Who was *Gladys*?" I asked.

"Yep, *Gladys*. That's what I call the old lady. Been driving her for ten years and she ain't never let me down. Named her after my schoolteacher, Miss Gladys Connors. She was one helluva woman. She used to lay my head between her thick thighs and cane my rump when I was bad."

"Let us waste no more time," Holmes said.

"Boys. Old *Gladys* needs a head of steam. You," he pointed at me, "get up and heave wood into the boiler. We all three climbed into the engine cab.

"*Gladys* can be mighty temperamental. She needs a full head of steam to get over that bridge before it falls down," Billy said.

The entire span was constructed of spindly timbers; the current in the Big Muddy River swept against the wooden pilings with a force that shook the entire creaky structure. It looked awfully dangerous, and I sincerely doubted that *Gladys* could traverse it safely.

Billy took a long pull at a bottle and offered me a drink. I could not say no to a fellow Irishman, so I had a long swallow, opened the furnace door, and threw chunks of wood on the fire.

"I presume you will cross the bridge slowly and with great care," said Holmes.

"Hell, no, that ain't the way." The fire roared and the steam gauge topped the last red mark. Billy put her in reverse. We chugged about one hundred yards away from the bridge and came to a halt. Billy took another pull at the bottle. "Let her rip!" he yelled.

Black smoke poured out of the stack. The fire roared. Billy let off the brake and sounded the whistle. "Hold on, boys!" he whooped.

The wheels turned faster and faster until we flew. I could have sworn we left the track. *Gladys* pounded down the slope, gaining more speed until we hit the bridge. Billy kept his head out the window with one hand on the throttle. His hat flew off, but he ignored that and gave another pull on the throttle. Sherlock Holmes, as excited as a wee boy, yanked on the whistle. The mournful cry sounded across the little valley, but did not drown out the frightful *CRACK!* of breaking timbers.

I closed my eyes, said a good Catholic prayer, and crossed myself.

I did a little jig. "Aye, boys, that was grand. The grandest thing, I ever saw!"

We were across and safe. I looked back in time to see crumbling timbers and iron rails splashing in to the Big Muddy River.

"Damn all, how am I to get home?" Billy complained. He turned obstinate, slowed at every village, tootled the whistle at every dog, child, and woman and refused to press on with more speed.

It was almost a quarter to four o'clock when we pulled into the Springfield depot. Holmes anxiously consulted his watch. We had nearly fifteen minutes to save the President.

The station agent listened to our story with a smile. "You boys are a talkin' nonsense. They's guards everywhere, but we ain't got no cabs. Iffen, you want to hear the President, you will have to hoof it, but the tomb is only two miles away. The whole county's already there," the agent said.

We set off at a brisk jog. I was in good physical condition, but after a half-mile, Holmes slowed to a bare walk. "My dear Doyle, it is up to you. Take the revolver and run!"

I tucked the Bull Dog pistol into my pocket and set off like a madman. I found a pace, ran well and fast, but my boots sunk into wet ground and I slipped on patches of melting snow. In a few minutes I passed latecomers and then, suddenly, saw the tall pointed obelisk of Lincoln's tomb where I heard snatches of a stentorian voice.

Hayes had started early. Was I too late?

From a distance, I saw four flights of balustraded stairs—two flanking the entrance and two at the rear. Both led to a level terrace where the President stood in front of an ornate parapet. Patriotic red, white, and blue banners and streamers fluttered from flag poles. Dignitaries surrounded the President. Hayes, in full throat, waved his arms. "We are gathered today to honour the saviour of our union," he roared.

Stern-faced Pinkertons with rifles at the ready were on guard in front of the tomb and on the balustrade looking out over the crowd. They were intent on protecting the President and seemed competent. Things appeared to be in order with nothing amiss.

I breathed a sigh of relief. The Pinkertons were on the job, and, besides, the country folks and city people were purely innocent.

A few thousand spectators were spread out on the grassy lawn in front of the tomb, on the steps, the terrace, the balustrade. A few young bucks had climbed the bronze statues for a better view. Far in the back, folks listened from open carriages.

The crowd clapped and hurrahed at the President's every statement. Enthusiasm was in the air. Venders wandered among the crowd hawking peanuts and popcorn. Children played tag in the mud, and young couples held hands. Even though the day was overcast, it was more like a jolly holiday than a national event. Her Majesty, Queen Victoria, would not allow such nonsense.

I pushed through the crowds on the lookout for Captain Hook, especially beneath the terrace because Emilie Droussard had said "below the tomb."

Nothing looked suspicious. All was festive. Did the telegram get through? Perhaps the Pinkertons had already found Hook and his accomplices.

I began to relax and idly listen to President Hayes, when someone brushed my shoulder. "Well, lad, have you observed anything of note?" It was Holmes.

"No, sir."

"Perhaps I was mistaken and there is nothing to fear," he said.

The clouds parted for a moment. "Sir, look over yonder. What a gallant band of horsemen. They must be farmers, late arrivals." The band came on at a brisk trot. I counted twenty or more men riding two abreast.

Holmes shielded his eyes. "How curious; they are accompanied by two large wagons and are riding with purpose. Doyle, do you recognize those types of wagons?"

"If I am not mistaken, they are the great Conestoga wagons used to carry settlers west to California. The first appears to have a load of baled hay," I said.

The wagons were a hundred yards away when the wheels sunk into a patch of deep mud. The drivers whipped up the struggling animals with cries of "Gee up!"

Four massive draft horses were hitched to each wagon, but the wagon wheels appeared to be stuck. The horses struggled forward and pulled the wagons to drier ground. One wagon came to the last row of spectators. The other dashed onto a small knoll in the back of the cemetery.

Holmes was suddenly alert. His eyes twinkled as if he were solving a ticklish chemical problem. "Those horses are under great strain. They sweat and are well-lathered. Their nostrils flare and, man, look at those deep ruts left in the mud. There is more than hay in those wagons. They carry a heavy load, especially the wagon moving towards the knoll."

"They are only farmers," said I.

"Doyle, those men are no ordinary farmers. They are expert horsemen."

"Yes, yes, of course. They wear slouch hats and peculiar long coats. Perhaps they are cowboys," I said.

"Those coats are dusters, perfect to conceal weapons. They ride like cavalry men." Holmes sniffed the air like a bloodhound and slapped his head. "Damn it! I smell gun oil. Those men are heavily armed. I was wrong. Droussard's last message was not '*below the tomb*,' but '*BLOW THE TOMB!*'"

"Bloody hell!" I exclaimed.

"Follow me!" he shouted, and set off at a run towards the nearest wagon.

President Hayes made a rousing statement. Amidst the cheers one wagon halted on a shallow decline almost in the midst of the spectators. The other continued to move forward and came to a halt.

We were within a few feet of the first wagon when the driver threw down the reins and pulled off his long coat. The uniform was old and patched, but unmistakably Confederate cavalry. The man was a veteran of many a campaign. He was a hard, grizzled man who wore sergeant's stripes.

At his side, in a brown scabbard, was a long, deadly sabre. He paused and puffed hard until the cigar jammed between his teeth glowed brightly. With frantic haste, he tore away the canvas covering and hurled bales of hay from the wagon to reveal wooden crates marked 'US ARMORY'.

With a long knife, he tore open one crate in the middle of the pile to reveal bundles of red sticks. The wagon was filled with dynamite, enough to blow up the monument and kill the President and thousands of innocent people. The confederate jammed a long fuse between sticks of dynamite, jumped from the wagon, and unrolled the fuse as he went.

Nobody, not one of that crowd, noticed. Folks whistled, shouted, and roared with applause at the President's speech. The noise was deafening.

"Stop that man! Stop him!" I waved my arms and tried to attract attention.

It was no use. I jerked my head at the sound of pounding hoofbeats. There, not twenty feet away, a fellow on a chestnut horse coolly took aim and fired his Winchester at me. I ducked, stumbled, and fell face down. The bullet made a small geyser in the soft mud by my face. I was up and running again, with bullets whistling in the air. Holmes was closer to the wagon. With a burst of speed, he dodged the whistling bullets and reached the wagon just as the sergeant put his cigar to the fuse.

The fuse sizzled and sparked. The enraged sergeant drew his sabre and swung the steel blade in a deadly arc. Holmes ducked and, with one motion, pulled out his meerschaum pipe and smashed the heavy bowl on the man's temple. The sergeant went down. In an instant Holmes snatched the sabre, sliced the burning fuse with all the élan of a clansmen in Bonny Prince Charlie's army and jerked the remaining fuse away from the dynamite.

Sherlock Holmes had saved the day.

The now-shortened fuse spluttered out into thin air and the dynamite sat silently in its box with an unlit squat fuse.

I ran towards the wagon but a horsemen riding a big chestnut stallion dashed towards us. His whip stung my shoulder as he passed. "Damn you both! Get out of the way!" he shouted. My attacker rode like an old veteran, a cavalryman. I realized, with a horrible certainty, that these men were hard core survivors of Nathan Bedford Forrest's troops. These were the villains we had been searching for across America.

As I leaped away from the next strike of his whip, the other wagon driver had parked his four-wheeled cart behind some trees on top of the knoll overlooking the crowd and the tomb. The driver jumped into the back of his wagon, tossed the hay to the ground to reveal the big, ugly snout of an artillery piece aimed directly at the tomb.

I had studied military weaponry at university and knew that a cannon of that size could send twelve-inch shells hundreds of yards in the air. If a shell of that calibre struck the tomb, the entire structure would surely collapse, killing hundreds of people.

"Use the revolver!" Holmes shouted as President Hayes paused between phrases.

The riders on now-frenzied, bucking horses dashed in a great circle while throwing off their long coats. Each one had a pistol in his belt and a repeating Winchester rifle in hand. Every man wore either a faded Confederate uniform or a red shirt. "Sic Semper Tyrannis! Long Live the South!" they shouted.

The crowd took notice and, though many people screamed and began running in different directions, some simply laughed and clapped as if this were another Wild West show.

The riders created a diversion with their shooting and shouting. Holmes with his long legs pumping, ran madly towards the second wagon.

By now, I had the revolver out of my pocket and, with great leaping strides, ran towards the deadly cannon. The officer, in the gaudy uniform of a major general, lit a match and leaned over the touch hole of the beastly cannon.

I was yards away when Holmes shouted. "Doyle, for God's sake, shoot!"

I had no experience with fire arms, but, with trembling hands, I pulled back the hammer and pressed the trigger. I missed, fired, and missed again. At the sound of my revolver, the Southern officer paused long enough for Holmes to reach the lead horse in the team. He pulled the halter; the horse balked, but, with frantic effort, Holmes hung on for dear life and turned the horse's head. The team pulled the wagon into a sudden motion. The general lost his balance and dropped the match. He fumbled in his pocket for another while the wagon made a quarter turn. He struck a flame and ignited a few grains of powder in the touch hole.

The cannon roared and shot flames. The great *BOOM!* rocked me back. The shell flew, but not at Lincoln's tomb. Miraculously, the shell crashed and exploded harmlessly in the cemetery to the north. Headstones, earth, and trees erupted in a great geyser, but no one was hurt. Holmes had turned the wagon away from its target. The President was safe.

My first thought was for Holmes, but he was flat on his face, unhurt. I breathed a sigh of relief when he opened his eyes.

The Pinkertons came at a run and roughly shackled the old major general. The Confederates fired wildly and charged through the crowd. When two of their riders fell, killed by the Pinkertons' intense fire, they hesitated, then galloped away. More than one farmer in the crowd blazed away with squirrel rifles and shotguns.

The undaunted President resumed his long speech. "Please, fellow citizens. The danger has passed. Let us forgive our Southern brothers —"

The people — all those farmers, city folk, veterans, and children, now stunned into silence — edged in closer with renewed interest in the President's words. Meanwhile, the Pinkertons and volunteers helped the injured into makeshift ambulances.

Among the gaping, church-quiet audience I lost track of Holmes but made my way closer to the tomb and noticed a poor elderly man with a white cane. He wore a black hat pulled low over his face and a brown coat, with long, ill-fitting sleeves that hung well below his wrists. I assumed he was a sad, blinded veteran of The Great War, perhaps injured at Shiloh or Gettysburg.

He stumbled, and my heart went out to him. He tapped his cane and limped a short distance towards the memorial. People stepped aside and made way for his deliberate progress. He stopped, pulled his dirty beard, and listened to the speech. He went on, slowly, but always towards the President. Perhaps he was deaf as well as blind. Something was not quite right, but I could not put my finger on it. The cane was brand new. The handle was unusual, too intricate for a poor man's cane. I instantly thought of a *sword cane*. No, the idea was preposterous. I could not let my imagination run wild.

President Hayes went on. "This is a great era, a time for forgiveness. Let us seek peace with our Southern brothers . . ."

The tap, tap on the marble staircase continued. The blind man was near the terrace behind the President when he stopped and cocked his head as if listening. I assumed the poor man was a disoriented or confused veteran. A Pinkerton guard watched him briefly, then looked away across the crowded field.

The fellow moved on, deliberately now. For the first time, he raised the tip of the cane as a blind man will do if searching for an obstacle. It seemed to be a perfectly normal gesture. At that instant, the clouds parted, and bright sunshine flooded the terrace. It was as if God had shed a beam on the President to bless his salvation from the would-be assassins.

The shaft of sunlight reflected off bright metal at the tip of the cane. Why was there suddenly new metal on the cane? Instantly, the pieces of the puzzle fell into place. I envisioned with great clarity the puncture wounds of the curare victims. The so-called blind man had pressed a button in the head of the cane and flicked out what I knew was a deadly needle. He was preparing to kill the President.

Even with that clarity of thought, I could not fully believe it until the man stopped his hesitant tapping and lunged towards the President. Where was Holmes? I watched, paralyzed with inaction when, suddenly I came to my senses. The blind man's right sleeve had ridden up his arm, revealing a hook instead of a hand. It was Captain Spencer, better known as Captain Hook.

"Damn you! Captain Spencer, HALT!" I drew the pistol, aimed, and pulled the trigger. There was only a sharp click.

The President, alerted by my frantic cry, stopped in mid-sentence, and, with unsuspected agility, dodged to one side. The deadly cane missed the President.

Hook turned his eyes, murderous with hatred. "You again? Damn you, boy!" He lunged at me with the cane held point-first. "Justice! Down with the tyrannical North!" he shouted.

I made a flying tackle, hit his knees, and felt his hook swipe across the top of my head. I rolled and smashed a fist into his groin. The hook slashed across my cheek. I made a terrific kick that snapped his femur. We rolled together down the steps.

The man was incredibly strong and was able to keep going despite a broken leg. I rolled onto my back and there, above me, he was poised to plunge the tip of his cane into my neck. I heaved him away and rolled down one step. Like a tiger, he was upon me again, but, this time, I grabbed his arm, and, with all my might, forced the poisoned cane away. He attempted to rise, but I kicked his broken leg. He crumpled, and the deadly tip entered his stomach. He had impaled himself with his own weapon.

In his last paroxysm, his mouth opened, and his tongue moved, but he could not utter a word. He went limp, took his last breath, and died, practically in my arms. His death came surprisingly quickly. I supposed it was because he had loaded the cane with an extra strong dose of the poison to kill the President. His eyes had the same pleading look I had seen in Carl and the poor rat.

I expected immediate accolades, but, much to my amazement, the crowd blamed me. "That's him! He tried to shoot the President!" cried the gathering crowd. A half-dozen Pinkertons pinned me down, applied steel shackles to my hands and feet, and dragged me away to a barred police wagon.

The cries hushed. President Hayes made a last comment about forgiving the South before his guards hurried him away to a place of safety. The Pinkertons roughly tossed me into the police wagon.

When we arrived at the police station about twenty minutes later, the guards dragged me inside while a crowd gathered outside. "Lynch the damn bastard! Kill the assassin!"

While the crowd screamed for my blood, the guards threw me face down onto the floor of a filthy, solitary cell. I was still shackled and beset by an angry mob. Where was justice? What a damnable country. I risked my life to save the President and my reward was to have the entire populace of Springfield wanting to hang me.

Where was Holmes? Was he, too, under suspicion? It wasn't until later that I learned he had gone off to send an urgent telegram to Angus Duncan. He did not know I was in a dirty cell.

It was a long, dreadful night. My hand still trembles as I write these words. On that cold stone floor, amidst pools of filth and chittering rats, I vowed to give up travel and adventure and settle in dear old Scotland to practice medicine and, who knows, maybe even write.

10 December, 1878

It was almost noon before the authorities identified Captain Spencer, a.k.a. Captain Hook, and later still before Holmes, with the aid of Angus Duncan, came to my rescue. I was never so glad to see his dear homely face. "Come now, young Mr. Doyle, you must be famished. Join us for a meal," Mr. Duncan said.

"Aye, sir. Aye."

The lynch mob had dispersed, the railroads were cleared, and Mr. Duncan's personal gilded railroad carriage waited to take us back to Chicago.

As we sat in the luxury of the private car a fierce northeast wind blew gusts of snow against the windows. The carriage creaked with the cold, but a crackling blaze in an iron stove warmed my bones. Our belongings were still in the Peabody Hotel, but Mr. Duncan shared warm clothing and provided a fine meerschaum pipe for my use. Its fragrant smoky aroma filled the air and, in between puffs, we imbibed hot toddies, ate fresh oysters, boiled shrimp, and a strange soup, gumbo, fresh from New Orleans.

After I could eat no more Mr. Duncan and Holmes relaxed over a fine sherry and read the latest newspapers. I selected a Herman Melville novel, *Moby Dick,* from Mr. Duncan's library and settled down in a soft armchair to read about the adventures of Ahab.

A few moments later, Mr. Duncan laid down his pipe and newspaper. "I am sorry to say, gentlemen, but the newspapers make no mention of your adventure. There is nothing to corroborate your story. I am especially doubtful of your ludicrous tale riding in a balloon."

"The agent in Cairo and the President's guards will surely confirm our story," I instantly replied.

"Ah my dear Doyle, you do not understand. The station agent and the train driver will deny us to their deathbed for fear they will be accused of taking bribes. The Pinkertons are so humiliated by their inability to protect the President that they have hushed up the entire episode. The American public will never know how a couple of foreign sawbones saved their President," said Agnes Duncan.

"How do they explain the explosives, the cannon, the armed men, or Captain Hook?"

"The Pinkertons claimed it was all good fun by a band of rowdies to celebrate the President's visit. The Americans fire guns and cannons just for fun. The crowd trampled Captain Spencer's body. The President was led to believe he was a harmless, poor old veteran."

"How can they obscure the truth? It makes no difference. Someday, I shall put it in a book for the world to read so they will know what REALLY happened," I said.

Duncan made a face, as if he had swallowed a sour pickle. "Mr. Doyle, you are a fine young man. Calm yourself. Would England admit that a couple of Americans, including one who is practically a boy, thwarted a plot to kill the Queen?"

That bit of repartee left me at a loss. Holmes put down his glass and picked up a leather-bound book. "Mr. Duncan, if you desire confirmation of our story, listen as I read from Emilie Droussard's casebook. She gave it to me as she lay dying. The first part is mostly a diary starting at the beginning of the war. She learned the fundamentals of medicine from her father, a prominent New Orleans physician, but gave up hopes of becoming a doctor when she married a dashing officer. General Butler executed her father on a charge of treason and a Union sniper killed her husband at Vicksburg."

"Clearly, she had good cause to hate the North," murmured Duncan.

"She became a spy for Nathan Bedford Forrest and, with her elegant good looks, she had access to Union officers in the border states. She passed secrets through Dr. McGillicutty, a Rebel surgeon who introduced her to Captain Andrew Spencer, one of Forrest's men. She, in fact, assisted McGillicutty when Spencer lost his hand. This re-kindled her interest in medicine, but, after the war, every medical school in America refused her admission."

"Women have no place in medicine," said Angus.

I disagreed, but did not argue the point.

Holmes continued. "She gained admission to a medical school in Switzerland and, there, she again met Dr. McGillicutty who developed an interest in the implantation of monkey glands to rejuvenate ill, old men. McGillicutty was far ahead of his time. His work with grafting skin to the victims of the Chicago Fire was outstanding, but unappreciated. His determination to carry on led him to the remote plantation to do his experiments."

"All that makes sense. But, so far, you have told us nothing of a conspiracy to restore the Confederacy," said Angus.

"I was getting to that. Captain Spencer, or, as he was so aptly called, Captain Hook, never surrendered. The government charged him with murder because of his involvement at Fort Pillow and would have had him hanged. Instead, he ran to Mexico, joined Maximilian's army, and later fled to South America."

"Yes, many Confederates fled rather than live under the Union," Duncan added.

"Spencer made a fortune in gold mines and, incidentally, collected a large amount of the curare poison from the natives. He returned to this country, but, like so many other veterans, was in failing health. That is how he came to be re-united with Emilie Droussard and Dr. McGillicutty."

"Then, I <u>was</u> correct. McGillicutty was involved," said I.

"Yes, McGillicutty's experiments failed because of his difficulties in anaesthetizing the animals. The monkeys became wild and dangerous. He could not find a dose that would allow the animals to live and yet keep them paralyzed for the surgery. Emilie conceived of administering the drug with a syringe attached to a long pole placed through the cages. That, of course, led to the poison cane that killed, silently, from a safe distance."

"Wait. When did they start to work on human subjects?" I asked.

"Well, at first they gave liquid extracts of the glands to Captain Spencer. Here is a quote from her casebook. *'20 minims aqueous extract of a monkey's thyroid gland injected into the Captain.'* A second notation one week later read, *'Captain is agitated, pulse 120, no improvement in physical condition.'* This failure led to further experiments with human glands."

Mr. Duncan took a long drink of this toddy. "Again, I regret saying this, but this whole plot sounds rather hard to swallow." He spluttered on his drink and had a long coughing spell.

"I know. It is representative of the horror of medical science sans ethics. For example, here is a description of their first 'specimen'. *'Male schoolteacher, carpetbagger, aged twenty-two years. Paralyzed with curare, thyroid gland removed while specimen still alive. Extract injected into Captain Spencer. Improved.'* "

"Was McGillicutty involved at this point?" I asked.

"No, Doyle. He objected to using humans and abandoned the project, but, Hook, with his renewed energy, recruited men for his rebel army. His efforts led him to Chicago. There, according to Droussard, is where they hit upon the plan to use railroad guards as their specimens. The men were all young and strong. In addition, their loss would weaken the railroad's security and allow for their ultimate attack on the United States government."

"Diabolical. I feel awful about my poor men. I must set up a fund to help their families," Angus murmured. "Well, gentlemen, I do apologize. Sorry for ever doubting your story."

"Good . . . Then, we shall be in need of this no longer." Holmes snapped the casebook closed, walked to the fireplace and, with a puff of his pipe, dropped the book in the flames.

The pages caught fire. Maybe it was all for the best to spare the country from another dreadful story of rebellion. For now, it was best to allow healing. Perhaps I should even destroy my own journal. I lacked heart, but promised myself that this journal would never see the light of day while I lived. Our exploits, and the American adventure, would forever remain a secret.

"Arthur Doyle. Mr. Arthur Conan Doyle?" We had just disembarked from our coach as the porter shouted my name.

I lifted my arm, "Aye, that's me."

The porter handed me a telegram from Carl.

Rufus is better. I must lean on Rebecca to walk any distance, but we sometimes go to the river and think of you. Jimmy is fine. We shall return to Rush, but you will be gone. Please write to us when you are home.

The telegram mentioned nothing of marriage, but deep in my heart I know Carl and Rebecca are meant for each other. I was pondering this thought when we reached Mr. Duncan's mansion. "How did you know the assassin was Captain Hook?" Holmes asked.

"It is rather elementary," said I. "Doctor Bell, in his clinics taught me to observe and deduce in order to make the proper diagnosis."

With that, I lay down my pen and close this diary.

~ Arthur Conan Doyle, student.

<u>Editor's Elementary Endnotes</u>

Sir Arthur Conan Doyle once said, "It is a capital mistake to theorize before one has data." And so, my dear reader, before you close this extraordinary manuscript discovered by my colleague, Dr. John Raffensperger, there are some historical facts that I believe you should know about the actual life of the real Arthur Conan Doyle, et. al.

Fact. Arthur Conan Doyle embarked on his medical studies at the University of Edinburgh in 1876 when he was nineteen and Edinburgh was the world's center for medical education and surgery. The university was renowned for its curriculum, which included studies of the humanities as well as science. Joseph Lister had transformed surgical practise with his discovery of antisepsis that banished infection from wounds and was the world-famous professor of surgery.

Fact. The impoverished Arthur Conan Doyle barely had the admitting tuition and was forced to periodically support himself as a ship's surgeon or an assistant to country doctors. He also earned money by writing short stories. In 1878, one of his professors, Dr. Joseph Bell, appointed Doyle to be his outpatient clerk.

Fact. Dr. Bell had contracted diphtheria from a patient while he was a house surgeon. The disease affected his vocal cords and his gait but did not prevent him from becoming one of the foremost surgeons in Scotland. In addition to teaching students and running his large personal practice, Dr. Bell wrote textbooks, edited medical journals, and was the secretary-treasurer of the Royal College of Surgeons. Bell was especially gentle with children and, when his term at the Royal Infirmary expired, he became the first surgeon to have a ward at the Royal Edinburgh Children's Hospital where he continued to operate and teach.

Fact. Bell could deduce a patient's occupation, nationality and place of origin from such details as the calluses on their hands, mud on their boots and their accent. With his uncanny powers of observation he made rapid and accurate medical diagnoses. In the position of clerk to Dr. Bell, Arthur Conan Doyle briefly examined new patients to make a preliminary diagnosis. He then presented the patient to Dr. Bell in the great amphitheatre of the Edinburgh Infirmary in front of medical students and house officers.

Fact. When Doyle became his clerk, Dr. Bell was 36 years old, sparse, lean and tall with an aquiline nose and black hair. He had long sensitive fingers; his gray eyes twinkled with shrewdness. This is almost the exact same description that Dr. Watson made of Sherlock Holmes during their first meeting at 221B Baker Street in *A Study in Scarlet*. Indeed, Conan Doyle ultimately confirmed that Dr. Joseph Bell was his model for the great detective.

Fact. The esteemed authors Robert Louis Stevenson and James Barrie were real-life contemporaries and colleagues of Doyle at Edinburgh University.

And so, just as we began this endnote, let us also end with words of our esteemed hero, the real Sir Arthur Conan Doyle. *"How often have I said to you that when you have eliminated the impossible, whatever remains, however improbable, must be the truth?"*

~ Prof. Richard Krevolin, Los Angeles, CA. 11:41 a.m., February 29, 2016.

About The Authors

Dr. John Raffensperger, a retired pediatric surgeon, read all of the Sherlock Holmes stories as a child, and by the age of twelve, was convinced that Basil Rathbone was the real great detective. Years later, he discovered that Dr. Joseph Bell, the "real" Sherlock Holmes, had been the first pediatric surgeon at the Royal Edinburgh Children's Hospital. This led to an interest in the role that Dr. Bell played in the life of Arthur Conan Doyle. Dr. Raff is a medical historian who has written medical articles, textbooks of surgery, a history of pediatric surgery, sailing stories, and three novels. He now lives on an island off the coast of Florida and is training a hound, Daisy, to howl on moonless nights.

Prof. Richard Krevolin was thrilled when Dr. Raffensperger brought him the only existing copy of the lost journals of Sir Arthur Conan Doyle. He spent the next few years editing them, and when he's not editing, he can be found solving murder mysteries, writing plays, consulting, teaching, and directing films. He is a graduate of Yale College and has several graduate degrees. Krevolin now lives deep in the San Fernando Valley where he can be found oil painting. More info about him can be found at www.ProfK.com & www.PowerStoryConsulting.com

Also from MX Publishing

MX Publishing is the world's largest specialist Sherlock Holmes publisher, with more than a hundred titles and fifty authors creating the latest in Sherlock Holmes fiction and non-fiction.

From traditional short stories and novels to travel guides and quiz books, MX Publishing caters to all Holmes fans.

The collection includes leading titles such as *Benedict Cumberbatch in Transition* and *The Norwood Author* which won the 2011 Howlett Award (Sherlock Holmes Book of the Year).

MX Publishing also has one of the largest communities of Holmes fans on Facebook with regular contributions from dozens of authors.

www.mxpublishing.com

Also from MX Publishing

Our bestselling short story collections "Lost Stories of Sherlock Holmes," "The Outstanding Mysteries of Sherlock Holmes," "Untold Adventures of Sherlock Holmes" (and the sequel "Studies in Legacy") and "Sherlock Holmes in Pursuit."